Inviting Murder

PRIYANKA NATH

Rupa & Co

Typeset in American Garamond by
Nikita Overseas Pvt. Ltd.
1410 Chiranjiv Tower
43 Nehru Place
New Delhi 110 019

Printed in India by
Rekha Printers Pvt. Ltd.
A-102/1 Okhla Industrial Area, Phase-II
New Delhi-110 020

Chapter 1

Prithvi Suri relaxed as he sat in his favourite chair by the window, the one with a view of the ocean. A dim fog clouded the morning scene. Buses, cars, bikes, pedestrians, hawkers, together created a symphony of chaos.

Prithvi thought with irritation: 'So much noise – even at this age I cannot find peace!'

Just then the door flung open and his wife, Asha, walked in with the same force, heading straight to the desk placed at the other end of the room. Hurriedly she opened all the drawers, shuffling through each one's contents.

Prithvi watched his wife – slightly hysterical now – going through the desk. A small smile crossed his face. Suppressing it quickly, he asked, 'What are you looking for?'

'Oh, nothing…just a list.'

'List, which list?'

Asha did not reply. Instead she walked over to the bedside drawers and started to look through them.

Prithvi turned in his chair and repeated the question to his wife.

'Asha, what list?'

Asha had gone by now through all the drawers. Sitting down on the edge of the bed she said: 'The guest list.'

'Why are you looking for the guest list *now*?'

She looked at her husband and said sharply, 'Prithvi, stop acting ignorant. You know what I am talking about.' She got up and looked around the room; as if talking to herself she asked quietly: 'Where is that list?'

'Really, I don't know what you're talking about,' Prithvi mumbled.

Distractedly Asha walked over to where her husband was sitting. She stood by the French windows without saying anything. *Something was not right,* she thought. Who could have invited her? She was not on the original guest list. Perhaps some changes were made, after all I was not taking care of that. I should have taken more interest. Now…now we have *this* and no one knows *how*. I should ask…. Who did…. Oh, that would not look good. Suddenly her reverie was broken by repeated echo of her name 'Asha! Asha! Asha!'

'Uhh…what…what were you saying?'

'I was saying the list is not going to make any difference now. What's done is done!'

She looked at her husband and wondered if he knew who was responsible. Almost screaming, she said, 'Did you…did you have anything to do with this?'

'With what?'

'Inviting Nita to this reunion of yours. It was your idea to have this reunion, in the first place!'

'I don't want to hear anymore about this. Such nonsense. You women over-dramatise everything. This is not your personal soap opera with unbelievable twists and turns every week. What does it matter who invited *whom*, she is here and that's that! Just do the needful.' He said the last with such finality

3

in his voice that his wife, who had just started to say something, decided it best to keep quiet.

Together they sat there, in the massive master bedroom of Sea Point Mansion, each silently thinking about that evening's 'Diwali celebrations combined with family reunion'.

Prithvi Suri was a tall well-built man in his fifties, with a handsome face and intense dark eyes. His voice and attitude when he spoke was always firm, precise, conveying the message that this was a man unused to being defied. He had suffered a knee injury a few years back, which did not heal well even after many surgeries. This gave him a slight limp; he used a walking stick for support even though he did not really require it.

Asha, his wife, was an energetic woman, who liked to have everything in control. She was tall, slim and all her movements had a swift grace about them. There was beauty in her middle-aged face, and distinction. Her voice was charming, and yet authoritarian.

'Don't worry Asha,' Prithvi said now, quietly. 'I can understand your fears and I'll take care of it, okay?'

Asha controlled a sudden impatient movement. Instead, she nodded her agreement.

'Ask Nita to come and see me. And…two more guests will join us for dinner tonight. Ask Aparna to take care of the arrangements.'

'Who are these two guests?'

'An old friend, he's here on some official business, and an associate of his.'

'Oh. Someone I know?'

'No,' Prithvi said dryly. 'It was a long time ago. Why all these questions – just go and do what I have asked you.'

Asha stared at her husband for a moment, then got up abruptly and walked out of the room without a word.

౷

In another bedroom at the Suri residence, Chirag and his wife Aparna sat, discussing their plans for the party.

Chirag was the Suris' eldest son. He was a quiet boy with a gentle face. He never raised his voice, was always obedient and spoke in a controlled tone giving an impression of laziness. He was tall like his father but not as well-built. Aparna, his wife, was a simple woman. Once a teacher, she had given up her job after her marriage and taken over the managing of the 'Suri Residence'. Organised and good at handling the household staff, Aparna always made sure everything was running smoothly.

'Your father insisted,' Aparna was saying, 'there was nothing else I could do!'

'Well, if he insisted so much, there must be a reason,' Chirag replied with quiet acceptance.

Aparna, trying hard to control herself, said: 'Do you always have to give in to him?'

'He's my father.'

'Oh, I know – I know!'

'He has always had his own way.'

'Of course, because you let him! Who doesn't like to have his own way? But you're going to have to stand up against him one day, sooner or later.'

'What do you mean, Aparna?'

Chirag looked so shocked she didn't know if she should continue or not.

'What did you mean?' Chirag repeated.

Aparna shrugged and, choosing her words carefully, said, 'Your father is...bossy. He's manipulative. And…and recently I've been feeling that he's a little…secretive.'

'He is just getting old.'

'And will grow older. When will it stop? He dictates our lives absolutely. We are not able to plan anything on our own! If we do, it's shot down.'

'Papa expects to come first. He's very good to us and he only has our best interests at heart.'

'Oh, really? *Good to us?* Are you sure?'

'Yes, *very* good to us,' Chirag said, his voice still controlled.

'You mean *financially?*' Aparna asked quietly.

'Yes. He doesn't question our expenses. You can spend what you like on clothes, on yourself, this house, and all expenses are paid, no questions asked. He bought us all new cars just last week.'

'Yes, I admit your father is very generous. But in return he expects us not to question him or his judgment. You're like his lapdog.'

'Lapdog?'

'Yes. That's what I said. His wishes are your command. You do what he tells you to do – sometimes I feel you *enjoy* being his slave. You have no say in anything. Your brother gets to do what he wants, even when he is no good at anything. But not you, you have no freedom...*we* have no freedom.'

Chirag was not a confrontational person, and the argument was making him uncomfortable. He spoke surprisingly fast: 'Aparna, it surprises me to hear you say such things about my father. It is so unkind — and ungrateful!'

'Maybe, but I'm tired of it. I can't keep quiet anymore!'

'For God's sake Aparna, please be quiet.'

Aparna fluttered her hand as if brushing aside what Chirag had just said.

'You know I am right.'

'Papa is so fond of you —'

'I'm not very fond of him,' Aparna returned icily.

'It's not good for you to make such comments. If he ever found out —'

'Oh, I think he knows.'

'No. No, you are wrong. He has told me many times, how much he admires you and your competence.'

'Of course, I've always fulfilled what he sees as my duties. Anyway, I'm just letting you know what my feelings are. I don't like your father. He has you entirely under his control. You should have stood up to him years ago.'

Chirag was annoyed and his voice was sharp when he said, 'That's enough, Aparna. Don't say anything more.'

She sighed heavily. 'I'm sorry. Maybe I'm wrong. Let's talk about our "Diwali celebrations plus reunion",' she said with a touch of amusement in her tone. 'How do you think your dear brother Deepak will react when he sees Nita here?'

Chirag squirmed uncomfortably in his chair, he didn't know the answer to his wife's question.

Nita was Deepak's first wife. Their marriage – which had taken place some years back – hadn't lasted long, not even past their honeymoon. Their decision to marry had been a surprise, and their separation, a bigger mystery. After their wedding, the couple had gone to Paris for their honeymoon. The day they reached, Prithvi Suri had received a call from Deepak saying Nita had suddenly disappeared. Prithvi rushed to Paris, and when he returned the only explanation the rest of the family got was that local police was investigating, but nothing had turned up. A shocked Deepak had left directly for America for a change, Prithvi had told them, warning them not to talk about Nita when Deepak returned.

Deepak had come back after a year; a long time for 'a change' some family members had secretly thought but never had the nerve to say aloud. He had since remarried and was trying hard to establish a career as an actor.

And now, Nita had reappeared. What effect it would have on Deepak, no one could guess.

'I don't know,' Chirag said with slight annoyance. 'Who invited her, anyway?'

'Yes, who could have invited her?'

Suddenly there was a loud knock on the door. Asha opened the door and said, 'Aparna, there will be two more guests at the dinner tonight, make the extra arrangements, please.'

Aparna got up and started walking towards the door. 'Yes, I'll see to it. Including Nita right?' she asked.

'No, no, apart from her. By the way – did you invite Nita?'

Aparna was shocked at the question. She replied strongly, 'No! Why would I – I mean – I don't even know where she has been all these years.'

'None of us know. So who...'

'We have been talking about it too, but can't figure it out.'

Asha walked over to the cosy little sitting area by the windows. Sitting down next to her son, she said, 'I think we should all just bear with it tonight and tomorrow, when it's all over, we'll deal with it. I'm just worried about Deepak and his new bride. Such a shock for them, and I don't know how Deepak will take it.'

'Should I call and tell him?' Chirag offered.

'No, your father thinks it's best to just "deal with it". And who knows, he might not come and that won't be good.'

'So we should just let him have this shock!' Aparna was appalled. She thought, this family is too much! How they all like to sweep issues that are unpleasant under the rug.

'I know it's not fair, but for the sake of the family and the occasion, we must. And we'll be there to take care – just in case.' Asha got up and started walking towards the door. Abruptly she turned back to Chirag and said, 'Let's hope all goes well.'

She walked out of the room without waiting for a reply.

⌇

Prithvi's mind raced, wondering how and what he was going to say to Nita. There was a soft knock at the door. He walked across, opened the door and said, 'Come in Nita. You've surprised us all.'

Nita walked in slowly and stood by the door, unsure what to do next.

The room they stood in was divided by a broad passage lined with four pillars on each side. The left side of the room was faintly visible through the sheer curtains hanging from the high ceilings. This was where Prithvi and Asha slept. The right side of the room had been converted into an office. A large mahogany desk stood there, along with shelves laden with books and a sitting area near the windows. The wall opposite the entrance had three large French windows, opening on to a beautiful terrace with a view of the sea.

Prithvi started to walk towards the sitting area near the window, saying, 'Come and sit. We have to talk.'

Nita walked over and sat down, facing him. She was a petite woman, with long black hair. She had a big mouth, a broad nose and big round black eyes. She had a calmness about her; her face rarely revealing what she was feeling. It was easy to feel sympathetic towards her, though.

'So, what brings you here?'

She looked up at him amazed and replied softly, 'You invited me. ...Didn't you?'

'I! I didn't invite you. How could I, rather *why* would I?'

Nita looked a little flustered. She just sat there, folding and unfolding her hands.

'But...but you...'

'I didn't do any such thing.'

'What would you like me to do? Should I leave?'

'No, it's too late for that. You made sure of that.'

'I didn't do this on purpose. I didn't want to upset you, that's why I made this trip as short as possible.'

'How considerate,' Prithvi said with cold sarcasm. He stared at her intently for a few seconds, trying to judge if she was telling the truth. He knew her better than anyone in his family. He got up from his chair and walked over to his desk, took out a cigarette, lit it and came back to his chair. He didn't sit down, instead he stood right in front of Nita towering over her.

'What do you want?' he asked.

Nita, taken aback, said, 'I don't want anything.'

'Drop the act Nita. Don't insult my intelligence. I'm the only one who knows your true nature. You cannot fool me.'

He kept his eyes on her – watching her every reaction closely.

She looked up at him, her eyes filled with tears. She opened her mouth as if to say something, but no words came out.

Prithvi looked away and walked over to his desk. He opened the second drawer on the left, took out his cheque book and walked back to his favourite chair. He placed the cheque book on the coffee table between them and asked, 'How much?'

Nita looked at him with anger, but she controlled herself and said crisply, 'I don't want your money.'

He smiled a little and said, 'My dear, that worries me. You don't want my son, you don't want my money. What *do* you want?'

She stood up and said, 'Not everyone wants something from you or your family.'

Prithvi started laughing. Then, stopping suddenly, he said, 'But some *do,* and that's a fact. Now, what you might want may not be material, it could be *personal.*'

Nita stood there, her heart beating a little faster. Would everything be all right? Would she be able to accomplish what she had come here to do? She had thought it all out so carefully, prepared for every eventuality. She *had* to succeed.

Her full lips curved up in a smile soft and submissive – a smile that said 'you win, I'm caught'.

'Yes, you are right it's personal. I thought after putting you all through so much, maybe, by accepting your invitation and coming here, I could mend things at least a little.'

She started to walk away. Prithvi got up and started to walk after her. He placed his right hand on her shoulder and said to her, 'Perhaps I judged you wrongly.'

Nita didn't say anything. That had been too close. But she had managed to cross the first obstacle.

They had reached the door and Prithvi opened it for her. Is she trying to confuse me, he wondered. It's so hard to trust anyone these days. If only I could get some sudden reaction out of her.

He smiled and turned suddenly to face Nita. 'It was a fine gesture that you came but I feel it's best that you don't stay here. I'll arrange a hotel room for you and tomorrow you can shift there. I'm sure you can understand why – it will cause too many complications.'

Nita was taken by surprise, she had not seen this coming. 'Umm, yes...no – I mean, that's fine.'

'Okay then,' Prithvi said with finality in his tone. He gently pushed Nita out of the door and closed it behind her.

Nita stood outside still dazed. She thought she had been prepared for every eventuality. Now it seemed she was not. She *had* to find a way to stay. This was India – perhaps she could appeal to their inbred sense of hospitality. She started to feel a little better, but she couldn't get rid of a vague sense of fear.

ſ

Deepak and Chitra had been on an extended vacation in Singapore when they got a call from Prithvi Suri, calling them back home to attend a family reunion. Deepak was an average looking man, with a refined air about him, and the most innocent face. His career as an actor was very average, but he always managed to have some work. He had gone to Singapore for a guest appearance in a film; Chitra – as always – accompanied him. After the shoot, on her insistence, they decided to stay back for a few more days. Deepak's father's call had, of course, to be obeyed, and so their vacation was cut short.

Chitra was a young, pretty, vivacious woman. She had moved from Delhi to Bombay to become a scriptwriter. As time passed, she realised how difficult it would be to make it in the film industry. Politics, back-stabbing, betrayals – they were accepted norms in the industry. Her being pretty did not help either; she felt no one believed she was capable of writing scripts. Instead, she was offered acting roles. Soon she realised it was stupid to refuse work and so she began acting, first in ad films then in television serials. After she and Deepak married, she decided to go back to her first love and began working on a script.

In the flight now, with an hour to land in Mumbai international airport, Deepak said, 'It will be good, spending Diwali with the family. We haven't done this for such a long time.'

'I wish we'd had time to meet my friends in Singapore. They were so eager to meet you.'

'They are your friends, this is family.'

Chitra lost her temper, blurting out, 'I am doing this for you – for *us*. They have contacts in the business. Why is it so difficult for you to see what's good for you?'

Deepak started laughing and hugged his wife. 'I know, I know. I'm sorry,' he said.

Chitra's anger melted away, but she was still a little uneasy. She wasn't sure whether she should tell her husband the real reason for her disquiet. She was sure he would think it was a joke.

They both fell silent for a few minutes. Then Deepak turned to his wife and said, 'There is something I wanted to tell you before we reach home.'

'What is it?' she asked suspiciously.

'Well…I'm not sure how to tell you this. Please don't take it the wrong way.'

Chitra turned to him more fully and said, 'What is it? You're scaring me now!'

'Well, there is no easy way to say this but – Nita will also be there at this family gathering –'

'– What?' Chitra shouted. Everyone sitting around them turned at the same time to see what had caused this sudden outburst from another passenger.

Deepak smiled at everyone to allay their fears. He turned to his wife and said, 'Stop screaming like that. Everyone will think I am trying to hijack this plane!' he tried to joke.

Chitra stared at him, refusing to acknowledge his attempt to be funny. She said icily, 'Who invited her?'

'Actually, I think…I think *I* might have – indirectly.'

'What do you mean?'

'What does it matter. She probably won't come.'

'Of course it matters. Tell me all the details.'

'What details?'

'Details such as how you met her. I thought you didn't know where she was.' Chitra folded her hands across her chest, waiting for a reply.

Deepak looked at her, trying to make a decision. Finally he decided it would be better to tell her everything now; if he didn't, she would make a scene at home and that would ruin any chances he had. Calmly, he said, 'I met her one day in our hotel lobby. She didn't look too well. We started talking and she was apologetic. Asked for my forgiveness and so on. I felt a little guilty – and sorry. In the emotional commotion, I think it came out.... Just to try and change the subject.'

She gave him a stern look. 'So that's how she struck you...someone to feel sorry for. That's interesting. And you felt guilty so you invited her. How noble!'

He said innocently, 'Yes. After all, I'm happy now and sometimes I feel a little guilty.'

She fell silent for a few seconds. Then murmured softly: 'You need not feel guilty, if anyone should, it should be her. She did what she wanted to do. And left you to pick up the pieces.'

He put an arm around her gently. 'You're so wonderful. There's no reason for you to fear her. You are all that matters to me now.'

Chitra looked away. All her instincts were screaming *danger*. But there was no escaping this, she would have to face it. Silently sending up a prayer to god for help, she took a deep breath and said, 'Well, since we have to go I suppose it's in my interest to prepare myself.'

∽

Sheil got into a taxi and gave the driver directions to the Suri residence. It was a clear day. People were out, buying gifts, crackers and sweet shops were buzzing with more people than flies. Everything had an air of festivity and joy. Sheil's thoughts were nowhere near happy, though. He was anxious and nervous.

His short visit to Bali had been filled with emotional ups and downs. Bali had been so beautiful, and today a part of him wanted to go back – leave all this. Suppose he were to go back there now.... He felt warm at first, and then remembered why he was here. Something had started in Bali and he wanted to complete it. His lips set back in a grim line. He wasn't going to give up now. He hadn't planned for this, but such chances, such opportunities, don't come twice. That fleeting reluctance, that sudden cold feet – this doesn't feel right, is it worth it? why put yourself in such dangerous position? – all these were only weaknesses. He was not a child, he was almost forty now, confident, ambitious. He would not back out. He would do what he came to do.

The taxi stopped and Sheil got out, asking the driver to wait. He walked up the front steps and rang the doorbell.

Joseph, the oldest family help, rose from his chair in the kitchen and walked slowly towards the front door.

The bell pealed again. Joseph frowned. Grumbling about the impatience of people nowadays, he reached the door, drew back the latch and opened the door.

'Yes?'

'Is this Mr Prithvi Suri's residence?'

'Yes, didn't you see the nameplate?'

Sheil was taken by surprise. 'I'd like to see him, please.'

Joseph shook his head doubtfully. 'Today, it's not possible. He is too busy.' Sheil pulled out an envelope from his pocket and handed it to Joseph. 'Please take this to him,' he said.

'Wait here.'

Joseph shut the door and went to Prithvi Suri's room.

Prithvi opened the envelope, took out a letter and began reading. He looked surprised. His eyebrows rose but he was smiling.

'My God! Today is quite a day Joseph,' he said. Then turning to him, 'Show the young man up here.'

Joseph nodded and walked out of the room.

A few minutes later Sheil walked in, looking around him a little nervously at the richly furnished room. Then spotting Prithvi, he asked, with an American twang in his accent, 'Mr Suri?'

'I'm glad to see you. So you're Kamal's boy?'

Prithvi and Kamal had been roommates in college. Soon after, not being able to find a suitable job, Kamal had moved to Canada, and settled down there.

Sheil grinned rather stupidly. 'My first visit to the homeland,' he said. 'Father told me to look you up if I ever decided to come.'

'Of course, of course. You did the right thing. Come here and sit down. Tell me all about yourself and your father. Are you here in India for a long visit or just a short one?'

'Oh, I have just got here, I don't need to hurry now.'

'Yes, very right, you must stay here with us for a few days.'

'Oh, no, please. I can't impose on you like this. It's Diwali today and you must have other engagements.'

'No, no, you must spend your first Diwali in India with us! Unless you have other plans?'

'Well! No, I haven't, but I don't want –'

'Then it's settled. Joseph?' he called out to the man who had been hovering around outside.

'Yes, Sir!'

'Go and tell Aparna we have another guest. And prepare a room for him.'

Joseph left the room in search of Aparna.

Prithvi looked at Sheil in amusement. 'So, you've come here straight from Canada?'

'Yes, that's right,' Sheil answered. They began talking about the country, and politics.

⌡

The doorbell rang again, a much longer and aggressive peal than the previous one. Joseph got up quickly but walked at his own pace towards the front door.

The doorbell rang again.

Such a rude way of ringing the bell at someone's house, Joseph thought, shaking his head. If it's someone who isn't meant to be here, I'm going to tell him off.

He opened the door and saw a rugged, unshaven stranger wearing dirty, wrinkled clothes. Probably here to ask for Diwali baksheesh, Joseph thought.

'Hello Joseph,' said the stranger. 'How are things around here?'

Joseph stared for a moment and then took a quick breath. He peered closer, the same bold attitude, square jaw, strong sharp nose, the twinkle in his eyes. It had to be him. 'Our little master!' he exclaimed happily.

Sagar, the youngest of the Suri children, laughed.

'Seems as though I gave you a shock. Why? I'm not expected, is that it?'

'No, no – this is your house. You are always expected here.'

Sagar laughed again. He looked up at the solid structure of the house and thought, nothing changes here. 'Same old oversized house,' he said out loud. 'Still standing strong though. How's my father doing, Joseph?'

'He's fine, just some minor problems. High blood pressure, common these days. Stays home most of the time. But he's doing fine.'

Sagar entered the house and gave his bags to Joseph.

'How's my big brother Chirag?'

'He is fine too. Very busy. Handles most of the office work since your father stopped going.'

Sagar beamed mischievously. 'He will be surprised to see me, no?'

'I think so.'

'Well – he won't be too happy to see me. We never got along that well. Oil and water, as they say,' Sagar said, as he marched right ahead to the living room on the first floor.

'I'll go and find everyone,' Joseph said softly and hurried out.

Sagar had walked into the room but then stopped abruptly. Staring at the figure sitting on one of the sofas by the window, he said slowly, 'I must be dreaming! Is it really Nita? You sure look like her!'

Nita got up and came towards him, smiling. 'Hello! I was not expecting to see you.'

'You're in my house. You should have expected to see me. I see you're not as good with your calculations as you used to be.'

She was about to answer him rudely, when Aparna came in, walking quickly. She walked straight to him. 'Sagar? Hello, I'm Aparna – Chirag's wife.'

Sagar hugged her warmly and then stood back, examining her smooth appearance and gentle manner. He approved.

Aparna thought, he is the best looking of them all, and charming even in these filthy clothes. But I don't trust him.

She smiled at him. 'How does it feel, being back here after so many years? Does it look different or just the same.'

'Mostly it feels the same but I can see some changes. Are you responsible for them?'

'Yes.'

'You did a good job. Chirag found himself a good homemaker. Lucky him.'

Aparna laughed softly and said: 'I believe he is.'

'So how's Chirag doing these days? Is he still being the obedient son?'

'I'm not sure if you'll find him the same or different. But obedience is still his mantra.'

Sagar started laughing. 'I'm glad you have a sense of humour. How's everyone else?'

'They are all here for Diwali.'

'Oh, a family reunion. My timing is perfect!'

'Deepak will be here any time now with his wife Chitra. Did you know he had married –'

She was interrupted by a loud thud. Both of them turned around to see that Nita had dropped the book she was holding. She quickly picked it up.

Before Sagar could say anything, he noticed some movement behind him. He quickly turned around. Chirag was standing there with an odd expression on his face.

Sagar went over to his brother with his arms outstretched. He hugged him but Chirag quickly moved away.

Aparna caught her breath. She thought, how strange! He never talks about his brother. Why is he behaving so coldly?

Chirag spoke at last, 'It's been long, what have you been doing?'

'Well, a little of this, a little of that and a trip around the world.' Sagar knew this would irritate his brother.

Chirag controlled himself. He had become good at this now. 'Well, at least you're home.'

'I think I am going to enjoy my stay here.' Sagar smiled and looked at Chirag then Nita and finally Aparna.

∿

'I thought I was on vacation,' Maya Aryan said as she walked into Charles Wright's hotel suite. She sat down and looked up at him. The room was chilly.

'Have some coffee,' offered Charles, as he walked over to his briefcase and took out a black folder.

Maya made herself a cup and sat back comfortably, waiting for Charles to begin talking.

Maya and Charles worked for a secret organisation called the Black Spiders, funded by the United Nations without the knowledge of any of its member states. There were rumours about the organisation floating in the UN gossip vine, especially after certain unexpected incidents. But they were never seriously entertained; the possibility of a secret organisation funded by the UN seemed too improbable, which made Black Spiders even more effective. In 2002, two like-minded colleagues had come up with a design of a global intelligence agency not bound by borders. Its mission was based on the hard truth that 'Everybody wants something' and their goal is to get that something, no matter how.

The secrecy of this organisation was its priority. Its ultimate aim was only known to those working within this organisation. And only nine people know of its existence.

Charles and Maya were the two most active – and the most effective – members of this organisation. Their success in solving murders, robberies, assassinations made them popular among those who preferred privacy and those who were not comfortable with the law.

Charles Wright, the chief officer, was also a retired commissioner of police from Ireland. He looked at Maya and said, 'What do you know about Prithvi Suri?'

Maya thought for a few seconds and said, 'Not much, just a few personal details. Let's see if I remember correctly. Family had a diamond business in West Africa. He catered to elite clientele, rich people from Europe and America more than willing to buy his high quality diamonds. But when the diamond industry became less tolerant, and after being robbed many times, he decided it best to sell and move here – to Mumbai. He is rich and intelligent. One of the first few people who cashed in on NRIs and their love for Hindi films. Now he has a network of theatres across the world showing Indian films. He keeps out of limelight, though. He married late, has three sons and one daughter who died in an accident. He was in the news some time back. I think his second son's wife had disappeared on him – on their honeymoon.'

Not for the first time, Charles was impressed with Maya's ability to remember details.

'Is that all?' he asked.

'Well, there is a local newspaper here – the *Midday* – which ran a story once. Some small-time underworld crook had made claims that Prithvi Suri was involved in the smuggling of antiques. He had also said that Suri made all the negotiations between the underworld and willing buyers. I don't know how true this is, but that's about it. Oh yes, one other thing. He lives in a beautiful mansion.'

'So that's the reason you keep up with all this information?' Charles joked.

'No!' she said emphatically, 'I just like it. I liked it even before I knew whose it was.'

'Well then you'll be happy to know we are going to the mansion tonight. Mr Suri has invited us to join him and his family for dinner. So be ready.'

Maya looked questioningly at him. Charles handed her the black folder and sat back while she went through it.

The folder contained a complete record of Mr Prithvi Suri: his personal life, his professional life, all his dealings – legal and illegal.

Maya closed the folder and kept it aside. She had become more serious now. She knew Charles would not waste time without a reason. So much background information, there had to be something urgent.

She looked at Charles, gestured with both her hands and said, 'Well, it's your turn to speak.'

Charles sat up in his chair and said, 'Two years back, I received a letter from an old friend. We hadn't been in touch for years, so the letter took me by surprise. Here, why don't you read it yourself. You'll get the idea.'

Charles took out a sheet of paper from his pocket, unfurled it, and handed it to her.

It read:

Tibet

1 October 2004

My dear friend Charles,

I must begin by apologising for not keeping in touch with you. But I know you'll forgive me, we always had that bond of understanding. Right now I'm in deep trouble and you are the only one I can trust with this information. I'll explain as quickly and briefly as possible, because there is little time.

I was working on a story about Buddhist monks living in exile all across the world. During our interviews we stumbled across something known as the 'secret caves'. The idea intrigued me and my team. We decided to explore further. Our information led us here – to Tibet. We didn't find any caves but we did find accidents. I have lost all the members of my team, some are dead, some have simply disappeared. And I am on the run. I am writing to you because there is a big possibility I won't make it back and you are the only one who can find out what happened and who is responsible.

In the event of my death or disappearance, please make sure my family knows the truth. I'll be forever grateful.

If I make it across the border, I'll get in touch. If not, then you'll know…

With warm regards,
Your friend Richard

Maya folded the letter and handed it back to Charles. Her mind had already begun to sort out bits and pieces of information that could be useful in this case. But she didn't say anything yet.

'I'm sorry. He didn't make it, did he?'

'No, he didn't. I found out a few weeks later. Official report said trekking accident. But we know how much truth there is in such cases.'

'What about his personal belongings.'

'He only had his clothes, a watch and an empty wallet.'

'So, how is this connected to Prithvi Suri?'

Charles smiled and said, 'Richard was smart, he knew his papers would never reach us. So he got

Prithvi Suri tattooed on his left arm. I didn't notice at first, when I was looking at photographs of the body, but on closer examination, I saw it. There's a copy of the photograph in the file. So I did some research on Mr Suri. Now the time has come to find out what the connection is between the secret caves, Richard and Suri.'

Charles picked up his cigarette case and offered one to Maya. They sat quietly for a few minutes.

'I know a little about these caves. I mean, there is no way to authenticate it. But I have heard about it.'

Charles was not surprised. Maya always knew something about everything. She called it her 'collection of useless knowledge'.

'Well then let's see what else we can find out tonight – 8.30 p.m.'

Maya laughed softly and asked, 'Is this the first time you are going to a dinner in Bombay?'

'Yes, why?'

'Because, no one here shows up that early for any kind of party.'

'But we will. I don't want to waste even a single minute. We might not get another chance.'

'Fine. I'll get ready and be here by eight. But don't say I didn't warn you when we show up and even the host is not ready!'

Chapter 2

It was mid-afternoon and the Suri residence was buzzing. The decorators had finished their job and were just leaving. Some members of the family were resting; some were busy with other preparations. And Mr Prithvi Suri was giving his sons a rude awakening.

'This is my final decision, no more arguments please.'

Realising that nothing they said would make a difference, his sons began walking out of the room. As they were leaving, their mother stepped in. She didn't look happy; gave a sympathetic nod to her sons but didn't say anything.

All three men left the room and headed in separate directions without saying a word to one another.

⌒

Dinner was served and everyone was seated at the table. Charles was getting a crash course on the festival Diwali from his host. 'After dinner, I'll show you our in-house temple,' Suri said.

'Of course, I would really like that,' Charles replied politely.

Maya, sitting quietly by his side, noticed that no one else at the table seemed to have much of an appetite, although the food was excellent.

Joseph had asked one of his daughters to help him serve the food. Age had made him weak and he found it difficult to carry heavy trays. Brita came in with the dessert tray and went around the table serving it. She was a young girl who couldn't help but notice the beautiful clothes and jewels the women wore.

She noted Mrs Suri's pale blue sari with silver embroidery, worn with delicate pearl and diamond jewellery. She is always so elegantly turned out, Brita thought, but the dress her daughter-in-law Aparna had on was too simple. She was in a plain off-white and gray salwar suit which made her look like a nurse to Brita. Now, Chitra – she knows how to dress. She had worn a flowing skirt with a beautiful form fitted embroidered top, and a long silk dupatta. And Nita – so she is the one who ran away – she has no idea how to dress. Really! A pink sari with blue jewellery! She looks more decorated than the house, Brita thought. But what did she know. For the men seem to be paying Nita a lot of attention. The new guests – the man seems to be under dressed, the way foreigners are. Now she is beautiful, perfectly dressed too. A black sari with a single rose painted across it. A bold design but she can carry it off.

Joseph was trying to catch Brita's attention but when he failed he walked over to her and said softly, 'Hurry up, I need you in the kitchen.'

Brita followed him out of the dining room. Joseph had had a hard day, and even though he'd had help, he felt very tired. He'd been looking forward to this day, the whole family together again, but somehow things didn't seem right. Everyone was a bit gloomy. Chirag hadn't touched his food, he didn't look too well either. At least the little master was chirpy; he and that Canadian boy were getting along. But Deepak worries me – he has a strange expression on his face. I have known these boys all their lives but never have I seen them like this. Maybe it's because Sagar came back; after all he has always been his father's favourite, something that Chirag has always resented him for. Chirag always tries so hard to get his father's approval, and now Sagar comes back and takes all the spotlight. And of course Deepak has his own reasons to be uncomfortable with Sagar. Everyone had thought Sagar would marry Nita, but he left the country and she married Deepak. And he had to suffer so much humiliation – poor boy....

Everyone moved into the living room after dinner. Charles and Prithvi were sitting in one corner of the room and talking. Sagar had offered to show Maya the house. He was curious to know more about this woman who looked too delicate to work with criminals.

Nita was sitting by herself on the sofa when Deepak came and sat down close to her. Without looking at her, he said, 'I need to talk to you. Meet me on the terrace in ten minutes.'

When Chitra saw Deepak sitting next to Nita, she had a sudden urge to go up and drag him away. Since they had stepped into the house, he had been ignoring her. She wouldn't let anyone see her weakness, though. But I wonder why he's avoiding me, or for *whom*. She felt relieved when Deepak got up and left the room.

As Prithvi left the room to take his medicines, Sagar entered with Maya, who was praising the house. Charles, Maya, Sagar, Chitra and Asha were sitting and talking together when the doorbell pealed through the house, twice in quick succession.

After a few minutes a middle-aged man in a police uniform stepped in and surveyed the whole room with a quick glance.

Mrs Suri walked up to him and inquired, 'How can I help you?'

Inspector Desai had recently been promoted and with promotion had come longer hours and unprecedented situations. He was uncomfortable now; this magnificent mansion did little to ease his nerves. He blurted out, 'Uh, we received a call from this house.'

'A call? About what?'

'Did anyone here call the police?'

They looked at one another and shook their heads.

'Inspector, you are not telling us what the call was about.'

Inspector Desai was puzzled. He thought, either they are all mighty good actors or they really don't know. 'Madam, someone called from this house saying there has been a murder here.'

'What!'

Everyone was taken aback and started to speak at the same time.

Inspector Desai raised his hands, trying to quieten everyone down. 'Please…please. Let me say something here.'

Just then a voice from behind the inspector said, 'What is going on here?'

The inspector turned to find Chirag standing behind him. 'I'm Inspector Desai,' he repeated. 'We received a call telling us a murder has taken place here.'

'There must be some mistake, Inspector. Surely we would know if someone has been killed here.'

'Well, just to be sure, can you tell me if all the members of this household are present here?'

Chirag looked around and said, 'No, some are not here. I'll see –'

'If you could ask everyone to come down that would be nice,' the inspector said.

While Chirag had gone to find everyone, Charles turned to Maya and whispered, 'What do you think? A joke?'

'I don't think so,' Maya replied. 'No cop would spoil his Diwali for a crank call.' She leaned forward and asked softly, 'Did you find out anything?'

'Yes, a story, half of which I'm sure is a lie.'

'Well, let's wait and see.'

Sagar stood up and, laughing, said to the inspector, 'I think someone has played a joke on you.'

The inspector was indeed beginning to feel a little foolish. He'd be the joke of the stations. 'We'll see, we'll see,' he said absent-mindedly.

It was then that they heard a loud crash from overhead, then the breaking of glass, a loud gasp and the banging of a door.

Everyone stood up simultaneously and rushed towards the door.

The inspector was the first one out of the door. He rushed up the stairs followed closely by Charles.

Running towards where they thought the noise had come from, they reached Prithvi Suri's bedroom. Joseph was standing there paralysed, one hand holding the door shut and the other clutching the door frame. He was holding the door-knob so tight, his knuckles had turned white. His eyes stared in disbelief at everyone standing around him.

Chirag moved closer to him and said, 'What is it Joseph?'

Inspector Desai moved quickly, gesturing for Joseph to step aside so he could enter the room.

Joseph quietly obeyed. The inspector opened the door and looked inside. Everyone followed him as he walked in.

In front of them lay Prithvi Suri, sprawled out on his desk, face down. There was a pool of blood near his head. The items on his desk were slightly disarrayed. Lying on the floor was Prithvi's walking stick, with blood on it. There was blood smeared across the desk and chair as well. Next to him, the safe lay open, all its contents strewn across the floor.

There were loud gasps and then a few voices spoke in turn.

'Oh god! What happened here!' Chirag said.

'Who...who could have...' Asha Suri said, unable to contain her emotions. The entire scene seemed surreal. Her nerves gave up. As she was about to fall, Sagar caught her and carried her out of the room.

Chirag didn't know if he should follow his mother or stay with his father. Aparna, guessing his predicament, quickly said, 'I'll go and stay with mother, you stay here,' and left the room.

The inspector quickly took charge. 'Ladies, please. If you don't mind, please wait in the living room for me.'

All the women walked out slowly, whispering amongst each other.

'This feels too unreal, like we're in a movie,' Chitra said.

Nita shook her head, 'It's just horrible, poor old man, hammered to death. He didn't deserve it.'

Maya was silent. She wanted to be in the room where the murder had taken place. She didn't want to waste her time listening to these women.

Meanwhile, in the Suris' bedroom, the inspector was instructing Joseph to bring his men, who were waiting outside, up to the room. When Joseph left the room, Desai turned and walked over to the body. He checked for a pulse as a formality and then spoke to the rest of them. 'I think it's best if you'll also wait in the living room,' he said firmly.

Chirag let out a meek protest but his brother told him it was better for them to leave and call a doctor. Charles decided that this would be the time to talk to the inspector.

'We didn't get a chance to talk earlier inspector, let me introduce myself. My name is Charles Wright –'

Inspector Desai interrupted him, 'Yes, I know who you are Sir. I attended that seminar on security where you were the chief speaker. It's my good luck that you are here today.'

Charles nodded his acknowledgment. 'If you don't mind, I would like to help with the investigations. Prithvi is – I mean, was – a friend and I couldn't just sit and do nothing.'

Inspector Desai was a little relieved. Having Charles Wright on the team would definitely increase the chances of solving this crime. Something that could only boost his career. 'Sure, sure, your input would be appreciated,' he said, trying not to sound too eager.

Desai walked around the desk and stopped in front of the empty safe. 'I think it's a robbery related murder. Someone came to this room with the purpose to steal – probably through the windows. He found Mr Suri, killed him, stole whatever he wanted and then ran off.'

Charles was shocked. How could the inspector come up with this reasoning based on *no* facts.

'What's your opinion, Sir.'

'Please, call me Charles.' He walked towards the windows and continued, 'Why hit the victim from behind?'

'Perhaps the murderer was already hiding in here –'

There was a knock on the door and two constables walked in. 'Call Dr Saha, the medical examiner,' Desai ordered one of the constables. 'Ask him to come here immediately. And you – go to the living room – ask the family to stay there. Don't let them leave till I get there. Is that clear?'

The inspector came back into the room to find Charles standing in the middle of a circle of papers that had been, probably, thrown out of the safe.

'Have you spotted something?' Desai asked.

'Yes...' Charles murmured. 'Just a minute, this is odd!'

'What is it?'

Charles looked up and said, 'Someone has gone through each and every one of these sheets.'

Inspector Desai walked over and looked at the papers, trying hard to understand how Charles had realised this, and what the significance was.

At that minute the door was flung open and Chirag Suri stormed in. 'Inspector! Can you explain why we are being locked up in our own house? This is not right! We haven't done anything.'

Desai knew he had to handle this tactfully. He said as politely as he could, 'Mr Suri, I understand. But as you can see, the circumstances are not normal. At this stage, *anyone* could be responsible for this.'

'What do you mean?' Chirag shouted. 'One of *us* has done this?'

'I don't know, we can't say anything yet. Which is why we can't let anyone leave the house.'

Inspector Desai looked at Charles for help. Charles walked up to Chirag and patting him lightly said, 'Come, let's go, I'll walk with you.'

They both left the room. Right outside, a little distance away from the door, there was a small sit-out area. Charles and Chirag sat down there for a few minutes.

'Mr Wright, is it true? What the cop said?'

'I'm afraid so. He does have a point.'

'But that could ruin us all.'

'Now, now. It can't be that bad.'

'You have no idea about our society. The minute someone finds out, we will be prosecuted, convicted and judged before our legal system does anything. All of us will look suspicious.'

'Yes, this is true, unfortunately.'

'Mr Wright, you are a detective. Please help us, otherwise things could really go wrong. Please.'

'Don't worry. I am already assisting the inspector, but I need you to stay calm. I'll try my best to find out the truth.'

Chirag was relieved. Then something struck him, 'But Mr Wright, we don't have much time.'

'What do you mean?'

'Well, our daily help will come in the morning, and they will find out. Then who knows who they'll tell. And being rich in this city makes you news. This is a complete masala *story* for them. I am worried about that.'

Charles nodded, thinking that the case would need to be solved by morning for *both* their sakes. 'What time is it now?' he asked.

Chirag looked at his wrist, but there was no watch on it. Surprised he looked around. 'I think I've dropped my watch somewhere...' he said.

'It's about quarter past one. Why don't you go to the living room, explain things to everyone and be patient. We only have a few hours.'

Chirag walked away, still looking around for his watch.

'Could you ask Maya to join me here?' Charles called out.

Chirag nodded and walked down the stairs.

While he was waiting for her, Charles thought, 'I thought something was out of place here, but for it to be this bad...'

Maya walked quickly up to him and sat down.

'So, tell me. What is everyone talking about?' Charles asked.

Maya said thoughtfully, 'Some are discussing this event, some its repercussions, some are trying to figure out who did it.... Mostly they are not pleased about being trapped in one room.'

Charles was not surprised. 'No one is sad, or mourning Prithvi Suri?'

'Now that you mention it, a few sad words here and there. But no tearful reminiscences.'

'I think we should go in now.' They both got up and went inside Prithvi's bedroom. Inspector Desai was standing beside the body looking at the wound on Prithvi's head. He turned as Charles and Maya walked in. 'Is everything under control?' he asked.

'For now,' Charles answered. 'But we can't let them stay like that for too long.'

'Yes, yes. The doctor is on his way. We should soon know a few more details. We can question them and then they can be sent to their rooms. But not outside the house.'

'Yes, I think that'll be best. By the way, this is Maya, my colleague. I could vouch for her. If you allow, she can be of great help to us.'

'Sure Mr Wright. The more, the better. We're a little short on help today. Holiday, you see.'

Dr Saha soon arrived and got to work while the rest waited, standing close-by, watching the doctor. He finished his examination and turned to his eager audience. 'I can tell you a few basics but nothing detailed. For that you'll have to wait for the autopsy.'

Dr Saha was short and slightly on the heavier side. He had a pleasant smile. He continued. 'He was hit by a blunt object, suffered massive head trauma and internal haemorrhaging. He was hit at least three times. Died at least two hours back, maybe a little more or less. Anything else you want to know, inspector?'

'Yes, one more thing. Do you think this walking stick could have been used as a weapon?' Inspector Desai pointed at the walking stick lying on the floor beside the writing desk. There were some bloodstains on the handle which the doctor noticed.

'Yes, it's possible, but then again, I have to wait and see – to be sure. There is a possibility though.'

Inspector Desai stroked his chin as he said, 'Is there a way to test the blood on the stick and the prints now?'

'Yes, I'll take it with me to the lab.'

The inspector thought for a few minutes and decided to let the doctor take the walking stick.

After administering a sedative to Asha Suri, the doctor left taking the body and the walking stick with him. Inspector Desai had begged him to do the autopsy and fingerprint check immediately. The doctor assured him that he would; he said he would call and tell him as soon as he found out anything.

⌇

In the guest room next to the Suris' bedroom, Desai, Charles and Maya discussed the details of the case. The master bedroom had been locked and one of the constables posted on guard at the door.

'I am sticking to my robbery theory. What is your opinion? You have been in the company of the victim and his family.'

Charles shook his head. 'I noticed a strained silence throughout dinner. It hardly seemed like a festive environment. They all looked stressed out. It was as if there was some simmering discontent.'

'You're saying this might have been a planned murder?'

'What do you think?' Charles asked, turning to Maya.

'I'll hold my judgment,' she said softly. I want to hear what the family has to say. Because I think they are the link.'

'You think, it's one of them?'

'Maybe. It's certainly not the first time something like this has happened.'

'Yes, you have a valid point.'

∿

Chirag and his wife Aparna came into the room where the inspector, Charles and Maya were waiting for them.

The inspector asked them to sit down. 'I'm so sorry for your loss Mr Suri,' he said.

Chirag, his dejected appearance like that of a lost man, said meekly, 'Thank you. It's really terrible. My father.... He didn't deserve this.... He was the most kind, generous....'

Aparna jumped in, seeing her husband's plight. 'I am sorry inspector. My husband has suffered a great shock – all of us have. But especially him.' She placed her hand on his shoulder, comfortingly. She looked at the inspector and said, 'You probably have some questions for us.'

'Yes,' Desai said, glad Aparna was not a weeping wreck. 'Could you tell me, Mrs Suri, who all were present in the house tonight?'

Aparna straightened herself and replied slowly, 'Yes. My father-in-law, mother-in-law, my husband,

and me. His younger brother Deepak and his wife Chitra. The youngest brother Sagar – he had come after many years. Sheil a guest of the family. Mr Charles and Maya. Oh, how silly of me. I forgot Nita.'

'Who is she? Family?' asked the inspector.

'Well, she *was* family, but not anymore.'

'Could you clarify that, Mrs Suri.'

'She was married to Deepak, but it didn't work out.'

'So they're divorced?'

'I suppose so. We were not told and we didn't ask.'

Chirag interrupted. 'Actually, inspector, we decided never to raise that subject to protect my brother.'

'Yes, of course. Understandable. Can you tell me who all from this list live here and who are visiting?'

'All three of us live here. But I'm the one who is here most of the time. My second brother travels a lot because of his work or just for pleasure. The youngest – we never know with him. He comes and goes as he pleases. Nita is here as a guest, so is Sheil. He's a son of my father's old college friend.'

'Ah, an old friend.'

'Well, we've never met him before.'

'Oh, I see. And you let him stay with you.'

'He showed up today unexpectedly. My father couldn't let him spend Diwali alone. He insisted that Sheil stay with us for a couple of days.'

Desai nodded. 'That takes care of the household. Now the domestic help. Mrs Suri, do you trust them all, or is there someone you might not approve of?'

Aparna considered the question for a moment before replying. 'I think they're all reliable. Most of them have been with us for years. Most leave at night; only Joseph stays here full-time, and he has been with us for more than thirty years. He's family and his loyalty is not even a question.'

'Anyone who has just been hired?'

'No.... Joseph's daughter Brita came to help with dinner today, I mean yesterday. She is young and a bit silly – but that's the worst I can say about her.'

'Anyone you might be forgetting?'

'Well, many decorators came in today. But they left in the afternoon.'

Inspector Desai made a few notes and said, 'We now have to come to tonight's events. I know it's painful for you, but I would like your account of the evening. Mrs Suri, perhaps you would like to go first.'

Aparna said in a low voice, 'Yes, of course.' But she didn't know where to begin.

Trying to encourage her, Inspector Desai said, 'When did you last see your father-in-law?'

She ran a nervous hand across her forehead as she said, 'In fact dinner was the last time I saw him. After dinner everyone went into the living room and I went to the kitchen.'

'Do you remember around what time that must have been?'

'Well – let me think – about ten-thirty or quarter to eleven.'

'What did you do after that?'

'I oversaw some household chores and went back to the living room where everyone was.'

'Can you recall who all were there, Mrs Suri?'

Aparna had a keen eye and memory. 'Yes, I think I can,' she said. She pointed at Charles and Maya. 'They were there. Sagar, Chitra, my mother-in-law, and I. Only five of us were there.'

'Do you know where the rest of them were?'

'I don't know. I didn't inquire either.'

'What happened next?'

A little exasperated, not knowing what it was the inspector wanted to know, Aparna said, 'What are you trying to ask? We had dinner, I went to the kitchen, went back to the living room and was there till you showed up with –' She broke off suddenly.

Chirag intervened. 'I think that's enough. She has told you all she knows.'

Inspector sensed an urgent need to pacify. 'That's all right. I don't need to know anything more,' he said, then turned towards Charles and continued, 'Unless you would like to know something?'

'Not at the moment,' Charles replied.

'Well then, if you can tell us when *you* last saw your father?' Inspector Desai asked Chirag.

'Same as my wife – at dinner. After dinner I went to my office. I had to call a few friends and business associates to convey my wishes for Diwali.'

'You're saying you didn't leave your office room all night?'

'Yes, that's right. It was only when you came and Joseph came to get me that I left the room.'

'Did anyone see you. I mean – come to see you.'

'No, why would anyone do that? We don't keep checking on one another in this house.'

'Yes, of course,' Inspector Desai said, wondering what to ask next.

Just then Charles spoke up. 'Chirag, can you tell us what happened during the day today. Something out of the ordinary did, didn't it?'

Chirag was startled. 'Yes, but how did you know?'

'Just a hunch, that's all.'

'Well, too many unexpected guests showed up today. We were not expecting some of them.'

'For instance?' asked the inspector.

'Nita. We're still wondering who invited her.'

'Interesting, why didn't you ask her?'

'It would be rude. It looked like she had been invited, we couldn't just throw her out. After all she was once a part of this family.'

Inspector said gently, 'Yes, I can see how difficult the situation must have been. But I must ask the difficult questions – it's my responsibility to your father.'

'Er – yes.'

'So, could you explain to me Nita's relationship with this family?'

'She was my sister's friend. Used to come here a lot. A few years back she married my brother Deepak, but she disappeared the same day they reached Paris for their honeymoon. Today was the first time we saw her since her disappearance. So you can imagine our shock.'

'Who else was unexpected?'

Chirag felt uneasy, he didn't want to talk anymore. 'Does it really matter?'

'That's for me to decide, Mr Suri. Please answer my question.'

Aparna came to Chirag's rescue. She said, 'My brother-in-law inspector – Sagar Suri. He had been travelling abroad for many years now and hadn't been to visit us all that time. You see, it's natural that we were surprised to see him. Pleasant surprise –' she added.

'Ah! I see.'

'How long was he gone for?' Charles asked politely.

'Six, perhaps seven years. I'm not sure,' Chirag answered.

'Mr Suri, can you tell me what your father placed in his safe?'

'Just some important papers, inspector. Nothing valuable as such.'

'You mean, no jewellery or cash.'

'No he used to say it was too dangerous.'

'Are you sure?'

'Yes, I'm positive.'

'Mr Suri, did you make the call to the police station tonight – telling us of the murder.'

'No, I didn't. Why would I –'

'I have to ask.'

'No, I didn't. I'm as curious as you are about who did.'

Inspector transferred his gaze to Aparna. 'Mrs Suri, would you have any idea where the people were, who weren't in the living room?'

Aparna frowned. 'Not really. Who keeps track of such details.'

'Please try, something you might remember.'

She said slowly, 'My husband was in his office, making his calls. Nita was in the living room, but later she wasn't. I didn't see her leave though. Deepak and Sheil were there for some time, but I didn't see them leave either.'

'One last bit,' Inspector Desai said, 'Do you know the combination of your father's safe, Mr Suri?'

'It's in my father's wallet. He always carried it with him.'

'Thank you. It would be better if we interview the other members of the house first. The ladies may want to get to bed.'

Aparna and Chirag stood up and turned to leave. 'Shall I send them to you?' Aparna asked.

'Yes, please. One by one, if you don't mind.'

'Certainly.'

She moved towards the door followed closely by Chirag.

∿

Deepak looked grave, but calm. 'Such a misfortune,' he said, a little theatrically. 'I cannot believe this has happened to us. It can only be the work of some crazy killer on the loose. You must be aware of many such kinds, inspector.'

Inspector was about to answer but checked himself. 'You think it's an outsider?'

'Yes, of course. Who else could it be?' Deepak asked innocently.

'And how do you think he got into the house. And how did he leave? And most important: what was his motive?'

Deepak just shook his head.

'That's your job, isn't it? And if you haven't noticed, there are several windows in this house. It can't be very difficult getting in.'

'All the windows were bolted shut. We checked. And it seems nothing is missing.'

Deepak cried out, 'But that's impossible. Next you'll say my father died of a heart attack.'

'No, he was definitely murdered,' said the inspector. Changing tacks, he asked, 'Where were you after dinner?'

'I went to the living room.'

'But you left the living room. Where did you go?'

'I went to the terrace garden on the roof – to see the fireworks.'

'You were there the entire time?'

'Yes.'

'When did you find out about your father?'

'I heard Joseph drop something and a cry.'

'You didn't make any calls?'

'No, I didn't. Wait, perhaps a few. But I called from the terrace.'

'What did you do after you heard the crash?'

'I ran downstairs.'

'Did you see anyone?'

'No, I reached last. Everyone was already there.'

'When did you last see your father?'

'In the living room. Before he left to take his medication.'

'And you didn't see him after that?'

'No.'

'Mr Deepak, did you know someone had called the police, reporting a murder in this house?'

Deepak's jaws dropped. His eyes were opened wide. 'Someone from here?'

'Yes, from this house.'

'But – I don't understand.'

'Neither do we. But don't worry we will. It's only a matter of time.'

Inspector Desai leaned forward a little, keeping his gaze fixed on Deepak. 'How did you feel when you saw Nita?' he asked.

'Shocked, that's how I felt.'

'So you didn't know she was coming?'

'No, absolutely not.'

'Okay that will be all. If we need you again we'll send for you.'

Deepak got up and left the room.

$\backsim$

Sagar Suri walked into the room, his back straight, making him appear extremely tall. He had a strong presence. His features – the arrogant tilt of the head and well-built physique – showed a striking resemblance between him and his father.

Even though he outwardly seemed confident, the investigating team could sense he was nervous. 'Well, what can I tell you,' he asked, hands outspread.

'When did you last see your father?' Desai asked.

'When he was going to take his medicine.'

'Where was that?'

'On the stairs. I went after him to give him his walking stick.'

'And where did you find him?'

'On the top of the stairs. I handed the stick to him from below itself.'

'So, you didn't go to his room?'

'No, I didn't.'

'Can you tell me what you did after dinner?'

'Yes, no problem. After dinner I went to the living room with everyone. After that I took Maya around for a guided tour of the house. Then we went back and stayed in the living room. Till you came. By the way, did you find out who called you guys?'

'No, we haven't so far.'

'Really! Are you sure someone from here called?'

'Yes, Mr Suri. We are sure,' the inspector said abruptly. 'You recently returned from abroad?'

Sagar replied quickly, 'Yes, as a matter of fact today itself. I thought it would be a good idea. But now I'm not so sure.'

'Why is that?'

'See what has happened.'

'You've been away a long time.'

'Yes that's right. It's been nearly eight years since I've set foot in this house.'

'You returned now, can you tell us why.'

'I had lots of fun, but I was getting bored. My father wrote to me and I thought this would be a good change. So I came. That's all.'

'Did you plan this to be a short visit, or a long one?'

'I hadn't decided, but my father gave me some responsibilities which made me decide to stay.'

'Permanently?'

'Well, that's what I had thought.'

'Did you tell your brother and his wife? Were they pleased with your decision?'

66

'I don't know about her, but he wasn't very happy.'

'Who?'

'Chirag, who else. Deepak doesn't have the guts to dislike anything. Chirag is different. He never liked me. I was father's favourite and he is mother's. But he always was the good son. Did as he was told, no questions asked. So you can see why he was not happy that I was planning to stay for long.'

'He was not pleased with your father?'

'No, he thought I would ruin everything.'

'I see, I see,' the inspector stroked his jaw, watching him.

'Mr Suri, can you tell me anything about Nita?' Charles asked Sagar.

Sagar smiled a little but then became serious again. He said, 'I can tell you one thing – she is not as innocent as she appears. She's cunning and sly like a fox. And you won't even know it. That's why I left her. Couldn't handle her manipulative ways.'

'So you two were involved in a relationship?'

'Yes, for a short period only.'

'How did she come to marry your brother?'

'I don't know, I've wondered about that. But who knows, she probably had her reasons. Is there anything else?'

Inspector Desai shook his head. 'No, thank you, Mr Suri, not at the moment.'

Sagar walked out of the room without looking back. The three looked at each other. Inspector Desai said, 'What do you think Charles?'

Charles shook his head doubtfully and said, 'He is quick to talk about other people's flaws. I wonder why.'

Chitra Suri walked into the room at her own pace. It was as if she was floating across the room on a cloud.

'Beautiful woman,' Desai thought. 'Deepak is a lucky man. But if he doesn't take care, she will leave him and find a better man. And it won't be a problem for her.'

Charles thought, 'Beauty and grace, a rare combination. I wonder what she saw in Deepak. He doesn't seem to be the best of the lot.'

Inspector Desai quickly got up and offered her a chair. Chitra accepted and sat down with a grateful smile on her face. She glanced at Charles and Maya, feeling a sense of security with them around.

'This is all so horrible,' she mumbled. She was terrified.

'Yes, yes,' the Inspector said kindly but impatiently. 'It's been a shock, I know. But it's all over now. We just want an account from you of your whereabouts this evening.'

Chitra cried out, 'But I don't know anything, we just got here today. Really! That's the truth.'

Inspector Desai squinted his eyes and said gently, 'Yes, we know.'

Chitra continued at the same pitch, 'I never wanted to come. I told Deepak this was not a good idea but he wouldn't listen. Oh how I wish we hadn't!'

Inspector Desai sighed, realising it would be best to ask direct questions if he wanted straight answers. 'Isn't this your permanent residence, Mrs Suri?'

'Yes, yes, it is, but we don't spend much time here. Only when my husband is working in the city. Otherwise we spend our time travelling.'

'So, you don't spend much time with other family members.'

Chitra looked perplexed. 'No, we do. Just, not a lot.'

'I see. Now can you tell me when you saw your father-in-law last?'

She thought for a moment and said, 'At the dinner.... No – leaving the living room.'

'So you last saw him when he was leaving the living room?'

'Yes, that's correct.'

'Could you tell me what you did after dinner?'

'I went into the living room and was there till you –' she pointed towards the inspector, '– came.'

'You didn't leave the room at all?'

'Well, maybe once or twice, I can't remember. But not for long – to get a drink or use the bathroom. Just normal stuff. How can I remember everything?' Chitra said, agitatedly.

'Quite true. It was a tough day for you.'

Chitra took a deep breath, forcing herself to calm down. 'Yes, yes, it has been disturbing.'

'And finding Nita here must have been a shock for you anyway.'

'No, actually, I had prepared myself for that –'

'– What do you mean you were prepared?'

'My husband told me she was going to be here.'

'How did he know?'

'He was the one who invited her.'

'Really? Tell me, how did she react when you met her.'

'She didn't say much, neither did I. We just kept our distance.'

'I take it you don't like her much?'

'No, I don't,' she said in a firm tone.

'Why, may I ask?'

'I don't know if I should be telling you this...'

'Don't worry Mrs Suri, we understand that this is just your opinion.'

Chitra looked at them trying to make up her mind. Then she said, 'I'm not sure if you'll understand, it's a *woman* thing. Maya will understand me better.' She smiled at Maya and continued, 'You see, there are women who put on this front of being fragile, dutiful, helpless. But they're really scheming little monsters within. The sad part is that a lot of people are fooled by the act. Nita, I feel, is such a type. I may be wrong, but I doubt it.'

'Is there anything else, you would like to tell us?' Inspector Desai asked.

'No... If you want to ask me anything, go ahead.'

Charles slowly got up from his chair and walked to one of the windows 'Chitra, why did Nita leave Deepak?'

'I don't know. Even he doesn't know.'

'She never said why?'

'No. She says she's sorry, but doesn't say why she did it.'

'I see. That'll be all Chitra, we won't bother you anymore.'

She stood up, smiled at them gratefully and walked out.

After the door closed, Inspector Desai turned to the others in the room. 'Well, at least we are getting some idea! Did you notice one thing: none of them have an alibi – except both of you! Nobody saw anybody else. How is that possible? It doesn't make sense at all. What do you think?' he asked Charles.

'I would say that each person's character is now slowly beginning to unravel. It's important in this case – each individual matters,' Charles said seriously.

'I don't understand, Mr Wright,' Inspector Desai turned a puzzled face to him. 'What exactly do they all have to do with the murder?'

'They all seem too detached from the crime. Why? Why are they behaving like guests and not a family that has just lost someone close to them — and that too in a gruesome manner. Something else is distracting them. We must find out what it is.'

When Inspector Desai continued to look confused, Charles said, 'I get the feeling they're all lying. There — I said it.'

Maya laughed softly. They both turned and looked at her. 'I think we need to find out why Deepak lied to us. He said he was shocked to see Nita, and his wife says they knew she would be here; that he, in fact, invited her,' she said.

'Yes, I think we need to clear up a few issues. Why do you think he lied to us?' asked the inspector.

'He probably didn't want us probing,' Maya said. 'But his wife couldn't have cared less.'

'She seems to be a jealous one.'

'I don't think she is jealous,' Charles countered. 'Probably insecure.'

Inspector Desai had a perplexed expression on his face. 'But we are still missing a motive. Why would someone kill Mr Suri, and who made that call?'

'You won't be able to trace it?' asked Maya.

'Yes, but that will take time.'

'And that we don't have.'

Just then the door opened and Nita came in.

∿

Nita looked solemn. Her demeanour was calm, resigned – almost unnatural. She sat down and looked gravely at Inspector Desai. 'Yes, what can I tell you?' she asked.

'Can you tell me Ms Nita, who invited you to this dinner? I believe your whereabouts were not known to the family?'

'Mr Suri invited me,' she replied.

'You mean Deepak Suri?'

'No, I mean the late Mr Suri.'

The inspector was not expecting this. He was slightly taken aback.

'How did he do that?' Charles asked.

'He knew where to find me,' she replied quietly.

'How?'

'He would have been able to answer that better – I don't know.'

The inspector had recovered himself by now. He took over. 'Could you tell us when you last saw Mr Suri – the late Mr Suri?'

'In the living room after dinner.'

'You didn't see him after that?'

'No.'

'Could you also tell me your movements in the night?'

'Yes, sure. I had dinner with everyone, then we moved to the living room. After sometime I went to my room because I had a bad headache. I rested for awhile and when I was coming back, I saw everybody rushing upstairs, so I followed.'

'Did anyone see you go to your room?'

'Yes, I think Joseph did. He was passing by when he saw me go in.'

'Ms Nita, how do you feel about this family?'

She looked up at the inspector with a kind expression in her eyes that said – they didn't treat me well. But she said, 'They are cordial. But I can understand their dislike for me. I haven't made it easy for them to like me.'

'You feel guilty?'

'Yes, very much so. But it's not easy to repent…' she said, leaving the sentence hanging.

'What were you expecting when you came here?' Inspector Desai said.

'I wanted to apologise, mend fences. But I realised I wouldn't be able to do it.'

'What do you mean?'

'I didn't know Deepak had married again. If I had known, I would never have come. I didn't want to create more trouble.'

Suddenly, Charles spoke up, 'Nita, Deepak told us he invited you.'

Nita looked at him blankly. 'But that's not true,' she said.

'Have you met him recently – or talked to him?'

Nita hesitated, and then said, 'No.'

Charles nodded and said, 'I see, thank you.'

'That will be all, thank you,' Desai said. 'You can leave now.'

Nita got up quietly and walked out, shutting the door behind her.

∿

Joseph stood silently, waiting for the inspector to say something. He was nervous. I know how the police work, he thought, it's always the servant. They'll definitely try to blame me. If only they knew how much this family means to me.

'Can you tell me when you last saw Mr Suri?'
Inspector Desai asked.

'At the dinner table, Sir.'

'You didn't see him after that?'

'No, Sir. I was busy in the kitchen.'

'Did you see Nita going to her room?'

Joseph thought for a few seconds and then said,
'Yes, I think so. She was going into her room when
I saw her.'

'Okay, now can you give me details of your
movements please?'

'After serving dinner and cleaning up after it, I
was sitting and resting. It had been a long day. Then
you came.'

'What did you do after that?'

'Chirag came looking for me and told me to call
everyone to the living room.'

'Did you find everyone?'

'No, I was going up to look for the others. Mr
Suri's room comes first so I went in...and found
him...lying like –' He stopped, unable to finish his
sentence.

'Yes, it must have been a shock. Then what did
you do?'

'Nothing, I lost my balance and knocked over a lamp. I came out of the room then.'

'Do you remember who reached you first?'

'No, I don't remember. I was too much in shock. All I remember is you asking me to step aside.'

'I see. How long have you been employed here?'

'Nearly forty years, Sir.'

'That's a long time.'

'Yes, it is. I have been very happy here. They are like my family now. The children were all born in front of me. I have raised them too. I would never do anything to hurt this family.'

'You don't need to worry Joseph. Your loyalty is not being questioned. But we have to do our work.'

'Yes, Sir. I understand.'

The inspector then asked, 'Was Mrs Aparna Suri in the kitchen with you after dinner?'

'Yes, Sir, she was. She comes in every day, it's a routine for her and now for us too.'

'What does she do?'

Joseph rolled his eyes up, trying to assemble every detail in his mind. 'She checks if the housekeeper has done her job right, gives her instructions for the next day, comments on the food

– sometimes good and sometimes criticised. She likes everything well organised and running smoothly –'

'How long does it take her to do all this.'

'Ten to fifteen minutes.'

'How long did she stay tonight?'

'A little longer than fifteen minutes.'

'She left after that?'

'Yes, she did.'

'Did she come back later?'

Joseph paused, looking thoughtful, '...Just to get a glass of water.'

'Okay, now tell me, did you go into Mr Suri's bedroom anytime tonight, excluding the time when you found him?'

Joseph looked uncomfortable. What can I say, he was thinking. Anything I do say will sound suspicious. He replied in a professional manner, 'Sir, my job is such – I go to his room many times a day.'

'How many times did you go yesterday?'

'I don't know. ...I don't keep a count. Many times.'

Inspector Desai turned to Charles and said, 'Do you want to ask anything?'

'How are you feeling?' Charles asked Joseph. Joseph felt a warmth and sympathy from Charles. He thought, he is not from here, perhaps he can see what others can't. He could help...

Joseph smiled gently at Charles and said, 'Not good, not good at all.'

'You must also be afraid that they –' he pointed at Desai, '– might blame you?'

Joseph nodded forcefully. 'Yes, and I didn't do anything!'

Charles said, 'So you see, Joseph, in order to help you we need to find the truth.'

'Yes, I know. But –'

'But?'

'More than for myself, I want you to find the truth for Mr Suri. His death must not remain a mystery. The culprit must be punished!'

At least someone cared for the old man, Charles thought. He figured this was the best moment to ask, 'Joseph, can you tell me, didn't you feel the dinner tonight was a ... a little dull?'

Joseph had relaxed a bit now. He nodded. 'Yes, I know, I thought so too. But it's not the boys' fault. They were not expecting to be cut off like that. They just didn't know how to react. That's why they were silent.'

'What do you mean, cut off?'

Joseph had completely forgotten that there were others in the room; he was happy to converse with Charles. He said, 'Well, I don't know the whole story but what I do know, I'll tell you.'

Charles didn't say anything, he just leaned forward to show interest.

'I had gone up to give some letters that had arrived for Mr Suri. When I reached the door, he was shouting, so I decided not to go in at the time.'

'You must have heard something.'

'Yes, a little.'

'Please – tell us.'

Joseph thought for some seconds. 'I heard Mr Suri say, "you are going to give him half, and you no more schemes and no more money for shopping". That's all.'

'You left then? You didn't hear anymore?'

'No – I mean, yes and no.'

Charles laughed softly. 'Did someone catch you Joseph?'

Joseph's jaw dropped in disbelief. 'How did you know that?'

'A lucky guess. Who caught you?'

'Mrs Suri. She came from behind, took the letters from me and told me to leave. Then she went inside.'

'I see, thank you Joseph. You have been very helpful.'

Joseph was about to leave the room when Inspector Desai called out, 'Could you ask the houseguest Mr Sheil Singh to come and see us?'

Joseph turned around to face them. He said, 'Sir, we have not been able to find him.'

'What? What do you mean? I'll get my men to find him.'

'But, Sir, they have been looking for him. They couldn't find him, that is why they sent me in here first. Otherwise he would have been here before me.'

Inspector Desai got up quickly and went out of the room with Joseph. Maya and Charles could hear him shouting, then talking on the phone.

'He's really lost his temper,' Charles said.

Maya smiled and said, 'Who wouldn't be? He is more confused now than he was sometime back.'

'Well? Who do you think did it?'

Maya looked at Charles with an expression that showed amusement and surprise. 'You are asking me as if I know!'

'You usually take a good guess.'

She laughed, remembering how many times she had done that. 'Yes, but this time it's ... it's –'

'Too simple.'

'Um, it *is* simple – but that makes it more complicated to solve.'

Inspector Desai walked in just then. 'Complicated to solve?'

Charles said, 'Yes, we were just discussing how complicated a simple thing can be.'

'How can simple be complicated. It won't be simple then, right?'

Maya said, 'The crime is simple but the motive is complicated. That's what I meant.'

Inspector Desai still didn't look like he understood what Maya was saying. Charles, realising Inspector Desai's predicament, thought it best to change the subject. 'Did you find Sheil?' he asked.

'No, he's gone. His luggage is also missing. I have told my men to keep an eye out. But I'm doubtful. We don't even know what he looks like.'

'Actually, he looks a little like Sagar,' Maya tried to help.

'I'll tell my men, but that's just so vague.'

'I know.'

'This is disturbing. It also means he could be the murderer. Otherwise why run away?'

'I know, that's what we're also thinking.'

'We won't know for sure until we find him.'

'Should we talk to Mrs Suri now?' Inspector Desai asked.

'She was in the living room with us all the time. I'm not sure if she can tell us anything important,' Maya said.

'She can tell us who gets the money after Mr Suri's death,' Desai countered.

'And she can tell us what Mr Suri was telling their sons when she caught Joseph,' Charles added.

Maya nodded. 'You have a point. Shall we go? She is in one of the guest rooms.'

⌢

Asha Suri was lying on the bed, propped up against several pillows. Her hair was spread out around her, lending her an air of sadness and fragility. Her face looked pale, and her eyes were red. It was as if she had aged overnight.

Inspector Desai pulled a chair up to the bed, and sat down. 'How are you feeling, Madam?'

'I... I'll be fine –' her voice trailed off.

'I know this is a tough time for you, but if you don't mind answering a few questions...?'

'Yes, please go ahead...'

Inspector Desai cleared his throat and continued. 'Ms Maya here has told me that you were in the living room after dinner and didn't leave even once?'

'Yes, that's true. I was interested in what Mr Wright here was telling us.'

'I see. One other thing Mrs Suri – and I know this might not feel right to you – but I have to do it.'

Asha nodded and said, 'Please, you don't have to explain. I understand.'

Throwing his arms around the room, Desai asked, 'Who gets all this after your husband's death?'

'Everyone gets a share, inspector.'

'But someone might be getting more than the others?'

'No, you see, my husband made sure of that.'

'He made a will?'

'Yes, a long time ago, ten years or so. He has divided everything in three equal parts and made provisions for me.'

'Where is this will?'

'It's with our lawyer. But I have a copy which he gave me. It must be in my room,' she said, starting to get up.

'Don't worry, we'll get it later. For now this is enough.'

Asha closed her eyes and lay back on one of the pillows.

Inspector Desai had not finished with his queries but he didn't want to look insensitive either. He spoke gently, 'Mrs Suri, a few more details and then I won't disturb you.'

Asha opened her eyes slowly and replied, 'Please, be quick. I don't think I can take this much longer.'

'Yes, yes, surely. Can you tell me who all were present in the living room?'

Asha was quiet. Then she spoke, 'I don't remember clearly, the people I recall being there with me were Sagar, Aparna, Chitra, Maya and Charles.'

'And the others?'

'They were there, but then some left. The rest I don't remember.'

'Mrs Suri, I have been told that during the day your husband had a confrontation of some kind with his sons.'

Asha was surprised but she didn't let it show. She said, 'Yes, he did. But that was just his way of motivating his sons. He didn't mean any harm. They knew that.'

'But Madam, you think so, but others might have taken it seriously.'

Asha replied in an icy tone, 'What are you trying to imply?'

'Just making observations, Madam.'

Asha stared at him and then looked away. She said, 'I want to be left alone now, if you don't mind. This is tiring.'

'Of course, we'll leave you to rest. If we need to know anything more, I'll come later.'

Inspector Desai nodded at his two companions and they walked out of the room.

⌢

Inspector Desai, Charles and Maya went into the study, each trying to make sense of the crime. Then Inspector Desai said, 'We should go over all the evidence again.'

Charles agreed. The inspector left the room and returned after a while with a small brown box. He kept it on the writing desk and started to empty out its contents, setting each item down in a neat straight line. Charles and Maya walked over to the table. There lay a single sheet of paper, a tiny piece of glass, a wooden coin and a Singapore dollar coin.

Inspector Desai was thinking, each bit of evidence points in different direction. Did all of them do it? Let's see what these two have to say. He probably doesn't know much about our Indian psychology.... Now she might have some good ideas to work with. But even then I'll have to do most of the work myself....'

Charles was thinking, this can't be all. This points in two directions, and that too not strongly.

Maya was thinking, this wooden coin doesn't fit in this case. Where did it come from? It's rare – they don't make them anymore. She looked closely at the markings on the coin and suddenly it dawned on her. This might be it! It is more useful for us than the inspector here. I need to find out more about this, but how?

Their silence was broken by the inspector. 'Well, any ideas on who could have done this?'

Charles smiled at him and said, 'What are you keeping from us, inspector?'

Inspector Desai burst out laughing. 'How do you do it? I want to learn that – and don't say a hunch.'

'No, I can see something in your pocket which wasn't there when you left.'

Inspector Desai quickly checked his front pocket and noticed a slight bulge. He smiled at Charles. 'Ah, you have a quick eye Mr Wright.'

'It's something we men of uniform get good at – you'll agree with me.'

'Yes, very true, very true.' Inspector Desai was flattered.

Maya smiled to herself, thinking: Charles is so good at making others feel smart. If only they knew...

Inspector Desai pulled out what he was carrying in his pocket. He kept it on the table in front of them. It was a white dinner napkin stained with blood.

Maya blurted out, 'Where did you find this?' She thought for a second and continued, 'Not at the crime scene, that's for sure.'

'No, not there. Any guesses Charles?'

'I would rather have you tell me.'

Inspector Desai cleared his throat and said, 'This was found in Mr Sagar Suri's room.'

89

'I see. So now we have one more suspect.'

Maya was busy looking at the small piece of glass under a table lamp. She did not look overly interested in the new discovery. When the men noticed her Inspector Desai moved closer to Charles and whispered, 'What is she up to?'

Charles whispered back: 'She's probably noticed something. She sees things better than you and me put together. A woman's eye –'

'– notices everything that's wrong,' the inspector completed his sentence, and they both laughed.

Maya turned around and said, 'Lucky for you that this woman is on your side then.'

The inspector gave a bemused smile, 'Sharp eye and sharp ears too. We should be careful of you.'

Maya just shook her head in amusement as she signalled them to come to the table. 'Come here, I want to show you something.'

They walked up to her and, each standing on either side of her, stooped over to see. Maya said, 'Can you tell me what this is?'

'A piece of broken glass,' the inspector replied.

'Yes, but from where?'

Inspector took the small triangular piece in his fingers, turned it around and then handed it over to Charles, who did the same.

'I think it comes from a wristwatch,' Maya said. 'The quality and composition is similar.'

Charles agreed, 'Yes, you're right. A microscope would give you a definite answer, but I think you're right.'

The inspector quickly took the piece of glass back and looked at it again, wondering how he had not noticed anything. 'We need to find whose watch this comes from,' he said.

'I know that Chirag has lost his watch,' Charles said.

'That's interesting. But we didn't find it in the room.'

'That's because someone took it,' Maya said.

'Who?'

'Mrs Suri, I think.'

'How can you say that?'

'Because I've seen it,' Maya declared.

Inspector and Charles stared at her, amazed. Finally Charles said, 'Well, are you going to tell us more?'

Maya had walked back to the sofa. She sat down, picked up a pen and notepad from the side table and prepared herself to sit more comfortably. She kicked off her shoes, and said, 'If you check the flowerpot beside Mrs Suri's bed you'll find your missing watch. And I suggest you do it now, before someone removes it.'

The inspector quickly got up and left the room. He was back in no time, beaming from ear to ear. 'I've found it!'

'Did she say anything?' asked Maya.

'She pretended to be shocked, but I could see it was a front.'

'Did you ask her how she thinks it got there?'

'Yes, of course I did.'

'What did she say?'

'Said it was not her room, how could she know, etc.'

'Complete denial, then?'

'Yes, straight don't-know-anything attitude.'

Maya nodded and then said, 'I think we need to put everything down individually and analyse the data. That's the only way we'll get somewhere. Otherwise we'll keep going in circles.'

Charles agreed with Maya. It was how they had solved several cases; also, this one could use some structure. Inspector Desai had never heard of making an essay out of a crime. He believed in old fashion leg-work and interrogation. He was always open to new ideas, though, so he joined Maya and Charles on the sofa. Maya handed Charles the notepad and pen. She knew this was his expertise – sifting the facts from the clutter of words spoken.

〜

'First we should re-construct the sequence of events,' Charles mumbled to himself. On the notepad, he jotted down:

11:15 p.m. – Prithvi Suri leaves the living room to take his medicine

12:30 a.m. – Inspector Desai arrives

12:40 a.m. – Prithvi Suri's body is discovered

'Have I got it right?' he asked.

'Yes, that's about right. Maybe a few minutes here and there,' replied the inspector.

Charles continued, 'Taking into account what the doctor said, Mr Suri must have been killed somewhere between 11:30 and midnight.'

'Yes, approximately.'

'Now let's look at each member of the household individually.'

Charles began writing and a good fifteen minutes must have gone by before he said anything. When he finished he handed over the sheet of paper to Maya and Desai, who read through it.

Chirag Suri

Motive: Fear of losing his share to his brother – parental favouritism

Opportunity: Plenty – no solid alibi

Evidence on the scene places him there

Aparna Suri

Motive: Protective instincts could turn deadly

Opportunity: Many

Shaky alibi

Deepak Suri

Motive: Unclear, but could be related to what happened in the afternoon

Opportunity: Many

Weak alibi; may be a lie (could not have heard Joseph's cry on the terrace; he was probably nearby)

Chitra Suri

Motive: ?

Opportunity: Slim

    Secure alibi

Nita Suri

Motive: ?

Opportunity: Yes, but strong alibi (seen by Joseph)

Sagar Suri

Motive: Money (half his brother's share).

Opportunity: When he went to give his father's walking

    stick.

    While giving Maya the tour?

Sheil Singh

Motive: Robbery?

Opportunity: Plenty

    Has disappeared from the house

Joseph

Motive: ?

Opportunity: Has maximum opportunity in his job

Maya and Inspector finished reading the comprehensive list that Charles had prepared. They handed it back to him.

Inspector Desai said, 'That's pretty good, I must say.'

'Thank you. Now I think we have a clearer view.'

'True. Now let's see,' Inspector took the list back from Charles and continued, 'now if we start with Chirag. He has no alibi, evidence has been found against him, his mother tried to save him, goes to show even she suspects him. Evidence however small is still evidence. He, I feel, is most likely our strongest suspect.' He paused for a few seconds, then said: 'And he had a strong motive – let's not forget that.'

Maya agreed, adding, 'If he did it, it was easy for him. He could have easily left his study, killed his father and come back. Easily!'

'Yes, it seems so. Doesn't it?' Desai asked Charles.

'His failed attempts to please his father for years could have reached a boiling point, when half of his share was given away. His patience could have snapped and ...'

'Hmm ... you are right,' the inspector replied thoughtfully. 'It could be a psychological reason. We must get him in here and this time put him to task.'

'No, I think we should wait just a little bit more. Let's discuss the other possibilities first. Then we'll talk to all of them.'

'Right, let's look at the others. Do you think Aparna is capable of something like this? Looks too prim and proper to do something this messy.'

'She *is* prim and proper, but that makes her a dangerous criminal. One that plans things well in advance, executes the crime without even flinching, and doesn't leave any evidence. She could do this –'

'What does that have to do with protective instincts.'

'Ah, yes. That, my friend, could lead to several theories.'

'Let's hear them.'

'Well, she might (a) know Chirag did it and is protecting him; (b) have done it herself to protect his interests; (c) have done it along with her husband; and finally (d) have done it and Chirag is trying to protect her.'

Pensively Inspector Desai said, 'She did lie to us about being in the kitchen for a long time. When was dinner over?'

'Around ten-thirty, ten forty-five.'

'So she left for the kitchen at, say, 10:50, right? Do you remember when she came back?'

'It was after 11:30, definitely.'

'Are you sure?'

'Oh yes. She looked at her watch when she sat down. I remember thinking that perhaps she thought it was getting too late, so I checked my watch as well. It was 11:50 or 11:55.'

'Hmmm…. It cuts things quite close, but it isn't impossible. She had nearly forty minutes.'

At this rate, Inspector Desai thought, we'll have more suspects and no answers. I asked for their help and now I'm trapped. Otherwise I would have made my arrests by now. To move things along, he said, 'Who's next? Chitra Suri? Now, she is a character — blew the whistle on her own husband. I wonder why he lied to us.'

'It's a bit confusing: he says he didn't invite Nita, his wife says he did, and Nita herself says someone totally different invited her. Who is lying and who is telling the truth?' Maya said.

Inspector Desai became even more puzzled. He said with desperation, 'I should put all three in one room and confront them. Someone is sure to break.'

Maya smiled and said reassuringly, 'Believe me, you'll get that chance.'

'I hope so.'

'We should keep that option as our last resort,' Charles intervened.

Inspector Desai didn't want to argue. Difference of method, he thought. He went back to the list and said, 'Nita – the mystery of the invited guest. Who invited her? She does have a strong alibi though.'

Maya added, 'I don't see a motive. She gets nothing out of this apart from suspicion. Her reason for being here seems innocent enough. But who invited her?'

'Even if you find out who, it doesn't give you a motive,' observed Charles.

'Right, so shall we say a minor suspect.'

'I think she'll be last on my list,' Inspector Desai said. 'Even if she came here uninvited, they didn't throw her out. This goes to show she was accepted – perhaps reluctantly, but nonetheless accepted. Good enough for me. Let's move to the next suspect – Sagar Suri. He does have motive *and* ample opportunity.' Inspector Desai stroked his chin, thinking, he is a strong suspect. Why didn't I think of this before?

He asked Maya, 'He left you alone for a while?'

'Yes, he went to get the keys for a rare books section in the library,' answered Maya.

'Did he take long?'

Maya thought and then replied, 'Well, not too long. Five minutes, ten maybe. Not more than that.'

'Was Mr Suri there when you came back to the living room?'

'Actually, he was leaving as we entered.'

'That removes one opportunity, but he still had a chance at the time when he says he gave his father the walking stick.'

Inspector Desai, Charles and Maya were exhausted by this time. Maya suggested they should take some rest or eat something.

Inspector Desai was more than willing for a break. But there was still one name on that list that troubled him. Sheil. He said, 'Let's discuss Sheil's intentions. Chirag seems to think the murder was done by an outsider -- a subtle way of saying Sheil must be the one. What do you think Charles?'

'He shouldn't have run away,' Charles said. 'It only makes him look guilty. Perhaps he went in to steal something, found Prithvi there, panicked and killed him.'

'Sounds about right.'

'But there's nothing missing,' Maya interrupted.

'Perhaps he didn't get the time.'

'That's possible,' she said. Maya was still puzzled over these deductions but she needed more information. She would have to find out for herself.

⌁

It was by now almost five in the morning. Charles stood on the terrace connected to the living room. The usual sounds of an early morning had begun – a few cars, and buses went past the house. The city was waking up. Maya had borrowed a change of clothes from Chitra. She joined Charles on the terrace dressed in blue jeans and long white linen jacket. She was carrying two coffee mugs; she handed one to Charles and started drinking from the other.

'This city never really sleeps – I've been noticing,' Charles said.

'It's more like this city never stops working.'

Charles raised his eyebrows quizzically.

'It's true. This is no Vegas. People here live to work not work to live.'

'It's tough, don't you think?'

'No, I don't think it's tough. To achieve big results big sacrifices have to be made. Today this city of Mumbai is what it is not because of some movie stars or its rich elite but because of them,' she pointed at the people on the streets going about their daily routines. 'It's their willingness to work and make compromises – travel long distances, work odd hours. That is what has made this city.'

'It's in the attitude,' said Charles.

Maya laughed softly and agreed with him. 'Yes, that's right, it's in the attitude.'

Inspector Desai walked into the living room and noticing Charles and Maya on the terrace, walked over to them.

Charles asked, 'Well inspector, any more news?'

'No. I still have four suspects. I'm at a dead end.'

'What do you plan on doing?'

'There's nothing left but to confront them and hope someone breaks.'

Charles asked politely. 'Can I ask you for a favour?'

'Please, Mr Wright, you are embarrassing me. Of course you can.'

'Could you give me and Maya some time to do some informal inquiries on our own?'

'You want to question the family?'

'No, not question. Just talk to them informally.'

'Ah, I get it. Go ahead. How much time do you want?'

Before Charles could reply, Inspector Desai's cell phone rang loudly. He excused himself and walked away to answer his phone.

Charles looked at Maya and said, 'Why don't you talk to the women? I'll handle the men.'

'Sounds good to me.'

Chapter 3

As the early morning light slowly brightened, Maya paced the terrace at the Suri residence. The house was solidly built with no architectural pretensions: a red stone structure standing tall on a tabletop piece of land surrounded by trees and a private road leading up to the house.

On the roof was a terrace garden. Little flowering plants grew along the terrace. There was a small fountain and a few benches placed around it. Maya surveyed the garden with appreciation.

A soft sound behind her made her turn.

Aparna Suri was standing there. She smiled at her sombrely.

'I was waiting for daybreak. Last night seemed endless.'

'Yes, it is truly difficult.'

'I've never been in a situation like this.' She sighed heavily.

Maya thought it best to stay quiet and let Aparna talk. After a few seconds Aparna said, 'Yesterday when I saw Nita, I thought that was the biggest surprise of the year. Who knew.... She always brings us bad news.'

'Isn't that a little superstitious?'

'I'm not the type who believes in such things. But I'm forced to wonder in her case.'

'Why do you say that? What else has happened?'

'Well, she was friends with Sagarika – Sagar's twin sister – who died tragically. Then Deepak nearly lost his sanity. And now this –' she threw her hands up in exasperation.

'Coincidences, but I can see why you feel like this.'

Aparna moved closer to Maya and almost whispered to her, 'I never understood why Nita ran off like that. She never explained – *no one* knows – and now she shows up after so many years.... Maybe you can find out why she ran off like that. Why did she marry him if she didn't like him?'

Maya paused and then asked, 'If no one knew where she was, who invited her?'

'Even we didn't know –'

'Nobody asked?'

Aparna looked shocked. 'No! We didn't know how to react. She took us by surprise. And then, afterwards, it was too late to ask.'

'Did Deepak know she was going to be here?'

'You know, to tell you frankly, he didn't look too surprised. He just kept following her around. Even Chitra noticed it, we all did. I could see the anger in her eyes. Chitra would kill her if she could.'

'That must have been unsettling.'

'Oh yes, very much so. Unsettling is not the word for it.'

Maya nodded, commiserating. Aparna continued, 'I feel bad that you're caught in the middle of all this – a cruel twist of fate.'

'Oh, please don't worry. It's not the first time I've been in a situation like this.'

'You've been to dinners where hosts have turned up dead?' Aparna asked, shocked.

Maya realised how her statement must have sounded. She quickly corrected herself. 'No, no. Not in that sense. We have investigated many murders, robberies, assassinations…. I meant it in that sense.'

'Oh yes, I see what you mean. So you probably have an idea who did this.'

Maya said gently, 'No, it's not that simple either. Each crime is different.'

'Well, I'm glad we cancelled the original party, otherwise it would have been a bigger mess.' She shuddered at the thought of it. Her obsessively organised self couldn't even bear to imagine the chaos.

Maya interrupted her thoughts. 'There was supposed to be another party?'

'Yes. My father-in-law had planned this grand celebration. Guests were supposed to come in from all over the world. Hotels had been booked, as well as caterers, entertainers, decorators…. I mean, it was going to be the talk of the town.'

'What happened?'

'Just one week back he cancelled it all. Just said he's changed his mind. We lost our deposits of course, but that didn't matter. If only we'd understood why.'

'He gave no reason for his decision?'

'No. Only I know how difficult it was to call everyone and cancel the party.'

'I'm sure.... How many guests had been invited?'

'Nearly a hundred and fifty, two hundred people.'

'That's a big party. So if he didn't give you a reason, what did you tell everyone?'

'I told everyone he wasn't feeling well, what else could I do?'

Maya studied Aparna and felt a slight admiration for the simplicity with which she executed her own judgment in this matter. She could easily kill someone and justify it with ease, and believe it too, Maya thought.

She looked up to see Aparna staring at a figure in the garden below. It was Sagar, stepping in and out of hedges and cluster of bushes, looking around the rocks that were randomly placed all around the garden with vines growing around them. Maya knew instantly he was looking for something.

'What is Sagar up to?' Aparna asked. She looked at him, her eyebrows drawn together, puzzled.

'He looks like he's exploring the place.'

'That's all he knows how to do. And his coming home was such a surprise. It's just too much for any normal person to handle, you know?'

'Don't worry, it'll be over soon. Then you'll feel much better.'

Aparna sighed heavily. To divert her attention Maya asked, 'Tell me, if you don't mind, what's the story between him and Nita?'

Aparna looked at Sagar who was now walking into the backyard. She turned to Maya and said, 'All I know is that they had something going on between them and then suddenly things went bad and it was over. He went off, tried a few businesses, but failed miserably. He's just not good at such things. Obviously, my father-in-law didn't think so, though. He kept sending him more and more money,' she laughed sarcastically.

'You probably don't know why Sagar and Nita grew apart...'

'Who knows, and who cared. She married Deepak and we thought – oh well!'

'Sagar probably didn't come back for the wedding.'

'No he didn't. Probably didn't even know.' Aparna suddenly seemed to remember something. Abruptly she said, 'I must go now, lots needs to be done today.' Without waiting for a reply she walked off briskly.

Maya stood there thinking for a few seconds. She didn't want to forget any details of this conversation so she replayed it in her mind, trying to recall as much as she could. This was something she actually enjoyed doing: replaying a scene in her mind, pausing it when she wanted, to analyse a word, an expression. Slowly she started to walk towards the door and down the stairs.

On the way she met Charles.

'Is it okay if I talk to Sagar? I'm working on a theory,' she said.

'Yes, of course,' replied Charles.

Maya walked away quickly towards the backyard. There she found Sagar sitting on one of the many rocks that lay around. They were the ones left over after the landscaping. She walked over to him and sat down beside him.

'I used to come here as a kid,' Sagar said. 'It's quiet and no one bothers you.'

'You always had an urge to run away and hide,' Maya said.

Sagar turned and looked at her, annoyed by her honesty. 'Do you always get into people's heads and ruin their little joys?'

Maya was amused. 'Well, not always. Sometimes I give them happiness too.'

'What exactly are you doing today?'

'That depends on you.'

Sagar laughed out loud. 'You're smart – trying to make me feel responsible. Which in the end is the truth, isn't it?'

'Yes, you are responsible for your own happiness or sadness. Simple karma theory – come on, you're an Indian, if you don't know this who will? Right?'

'Absolutely right!'

They smiled at each other. Becoming a little serious Sagar asked, 'Do you know who did it?'

'Not yet, but things don't look very good for you.'

Sagar was silent. He knew it was not easy to convince someone of your innocence. Especially when you are not as innocent as you might like to be. 'That bad?' he asked.

'Well, we still have to wait for some more details.'

'I didn't do it you know.'

'Actually I don't know. You had the opportunity.'

Sagar got up in anger and started to pace in front of Maya. She continued to sit there calmly, outwardly showing unconcern.

'This is just my luck. Wherever I go it follows me around,' he said angrily.

'I think it's best you sit down. You'll need your strength for later.'

She smiled but quickly stopped when she saw he was not amused. 'Oh be a sport,' she said. 'Have a sense of humour.'

'Sense of humour! Sense of humour?'

She remained quiet. She wanted him to lose control a bit; it would be easier to get information out of him then. Sagar, almost talking to himself, said, 'I shouldn't have listened to the old man. Should have just stayed away – would have been much better.'

'Then why did you come? And don't tell me because your father asked you to. If that were true, you would have come back a long time ago. So why did you come back now?'

Sagar was silent, staring straight ahead at the mansion. Without moving his gaze he said, 'You won't believe me. I actually missed the place.'

Maya continued to look at him. 'It's not easy to confess,' he continued. 'Everyone has just assumed that I hate being here. But that's not true. Just because I don't stay here much that doesn't mean

I hate it. Nobody understands – it's not the house or the people, it's the idea that I run from. The idea of being trapped for life like Chirag. He was always trapped and now his wife is too. But I didn't want that for me. And I couldn't be like Deepak, trying to balance both – freedom and control. I wanted to make a choice, freedom. And I've paid the price for it too.'

'So why change now?'

'I'm tired. I feel lost and home is the best place to be right now.'

'Yes, I can understand that.'

Sagar was silent again. He wondered why he was telling her all this. She was a stranger, why would she care how he felt. He felt she was someone he could confide in, though.

Maya decided to change the subject. She asked, 'Do you know why Nita left Deepak on their honeymoon.'

The question brought a smile to his face. 'How is that important?'

'Everything is.'

'To tell you the truth, I don't know why she married him in the first place. She was never really fond of him. At least I didn't notice any particular affection on her side.'

'Couldn't that just be jealousy?'

'Please, hardly. I was relieved more than anything.'

'Relieved that it was not you who had to suffer the trauma of being abandoned?'

'Something like that.' A soft smile hovered on his lips though it was obvious he was trying to suppress it.

Maya noticed; she understood only too well the need to be carefree even in an inappropriate environment.

She said, 'You can smile – I won't tell anyone.'

He started laughing and said, 'This doesn't make me look very good does it?'

'Well, we all have our weak moments.'

Sagar fell silent. That sentence probably had more to it, he thought. 'What are you trying to hint at?' he asked.

'I'm not hinting at anything. If I have something to say, I just come out and say it. I'm not the type who hints. It's a waste of time. What I was wondering is, everyone wants to know why Nita left Deepak, but what I want to know is why *you* left her?'

'It wasn't one thing in particular really. We just stopped calling one another – or rather, she stopped calling me. And it ended. Just like that.'

'If it was that easy, why did you run away?'

'Who says I ran away!'

'So you probably didn't know about your brother's engagement to her?'

'No, actually I didn't, and even if I did that wouldn't have changed anything. He would never have listened to me.'

'You would have tried to stop him?'

'I would have tried to, at least, after all he's my brother. But to be honest I wouldn't have broken my back over it. If he insists on ruining his life he is welcome to it.'

'Well you must be glad now since he has married again.'

'Yeah I was, but…'

'But what?' ·

'Well, I don't know –' he didn't want to make any guesses. What if he was wrong.

'You know, your brother lied about Nita. He told us he didn't invite her, and she says he didn't invite her, but Chitra says otherwise. Do you know who is lying?'

'I don't know. How should I?'

'I think it's time to start answering some questions. Otherwise it won't be long before you are —'

Sagar was shocked. 'What? What are you saying!'

'You heard me. I'm trying to figure it out but who knows....'

Maya left him standing there, wondering about his fate.

∿

Time was ticking away fast and there was little solution in sight. Maya walked aimlessly around the house and stopped in front of a huge wooden door encrusted with dozens of tiny bells. Joseph was standing in front of the door, staring at it blankly.

Maya moved closer to him. He became aware of her presence and turned around. 'I was about to go in and clean.'

'If you don't mind, I'll join you.'

Joseph nodded and opened the door. The bells tinkled and quietly died down. It made Maya feel like she was entering the gates of paradise. Maya had always wondered why there were bells in temples.

When she finally got her answer it really appealed to her – the bells made one forget everything; it brought one into the present, the moment.

She looked around the decorated room, with its elaborate altar, and said, 'It is beautiful in here, and so peaceful.'

'Yes, it is. Sir had it made especially for his mother.'

Joseph was silent for some time, while Maya sat down on one of the cushions there. She needed to come up with a new strategy soon, or it could end badly. Plus they hadn't gotten anywhere with the work they had actually come here for.

Joseph interrupted her chain of thoughts. 'Can I ask you something, Madam?'

'Sure, Joseph,' Maya said, sitting up. 'Go ahead.'

'Can you tell me how Sir died?'

'You don't know?'

'No, who would tell me?'

'He died of head injury.'

'You mean somebody hit him on his head and he died because of that?'

Maya nodded.

'I see, so he was hit on the head.'

'Yes, he was – three times or maybe more.'

'Oh my god. Poor man, hammered to death. It's terrible. I hope you find who did this and make sure he rots in jail.'

'We are trying our best,' Maya said, but her mind was on something else; something that had struck her as familiar.

Joseph continued, 'Do you have any idea who...?'

'No, not yet.'

'You think it's one of the family?'

'Maybe. What do you think? You have known them for years.'

'Well, they are an odd bunch but not violent. I don't think it's one of them. Unless you find out the truth everyone is under suspicion. And god only knows what our police will find out. Nothing is safe with them. You know what I mean?'

'Yes, I know,' Maya said.

'If only someone had been there, happened to see the murderer —'

'I know. By the way, you told us you saw Nita going into her room. What time was that?'

'I'm not sure.'

'Do you remember anything else — anything at all?'

Joseph thought for a few seconds and said, 'No, I don't think so. I stayed in the kitchen most of the time.'

'You think the boys were so upset that they would do such a thing.'

'No, it's not the boys…. Somebody is trying to destroy everything that this family has built,' he said loudly and protectively.

Maya didn't want to argue with him. 'Joseph can you tell me – your opinion only – who do you think Deepak is more happy with, Nita or Chitra.'

Joseph was uncomfortable; his morals would never have allowed him to answer this question in any other circumstance. But, now, he wanted to help.

'I think – Nita.'

'Really? Why do you say that?'

'Well these eyes have seen a lot. And to tell who likes whom or who's happy with whom is not so hard to tell.'

'If that's true why did he marry again?'

'Who knows? Anyway everyone deserves a second chance. And why shouldn't he be happy.'

'But he might not be happy after all. If you're right.'

Joseph shrugged and returned to cleaning the altar. 'Well, we can only try. The rest is in god's hands. What else can I say.'

'I agree, it's all in his hands in the end.'

Maya looked at the altar, thinking. Her mind was trying to figure out what Joseph had said that had struck her as familiar. She walked out of the room and went looking for Inspector Desai and Charles, hoping that they at least had some new information.

∿

At that moment, Charles was sitting with Chirag in the latter's study. It was a small room with a desk and two leather easy chairs, in which they were sitting, facing each other:

'It's best you tell me what happened that afternoon,' Charles said. 'Your mother tried to hide it, but things like these do come out sooner or later.'

Chirag thought for a moment then said. 'He was angry at us for not being up to the mark. He often was, so it was nothing more serious than usual. But my youngest brother's return made my father feel that everything would be all right now.'

'And you didn't agree?'

'Of course not. My brother knows nothing about the business. He is a wanderer. He would ruin everything and then run away.'

'He always does that?'

'Oh yes. When things get tough or responsibilities increase he goes flying out of here. He has no sense of commitment.'

'That's why he left Nita?'

Chirag was stunned. 'Who told you about him and Nita?'

'Like I said, these things do come out.'

'We never really knew why – he didn't tell and we didn't ask.'

'Do you know why she left Deepak?'

'No, we don't know that either.'

'Can you guess?'

Chirag thought and said, 'Maybe... maybe she realised she made the wrong choice.'

'But why wait till so late to end the relationship.'

'Who knows what women do these days.' Chirag sounded confused.

'Don't you find it odd that you don't know anything about anyone in your own family?'

'These are unimportant things. And sometimes it's best not to know anything.'

'It could lead to a break down and a situation such as the one your family is in now.'

'You think we're responsible?'

'Why? Do you see any other possibility?'

'What about that guy – Sheil? We don't know anything about him. He could have been an impostor. And now he has vanished. Don't you think it looks like he's guilty?'

Charles knew Chirag had a valid point. But he also knew how people would try anything to pin blame on others to save their own skin. Chirag, in turn, sensed that Charles suspected the motive behind his accusation against Sheil, but he knew he had to insist on it – there could be no other explanation. Perhaps asking this man to help us was not such a good idea, he thought.

Charles continued to look at Chirag. He does look guilty of something, but the evidence must be there to prove it, he thought.

'What does the evidence indicate now?' Chirag asked.

'It points to all of you.' At Chirag's puzzled look, Charles continued, 'What I meant was, right now it looks like any one of you could have done it. Most

122

of you have no alibi. And the evidence points towards everyone.'

'How is that possible? *All* of us couldn't have done it!'

'I know it's not likely, but this is what the evidence shows, and the possibility cannot be eliminated.'

'But you were going to help us –' Chirag said innocently.

Charles leaned a little forward and – looking straight into Chirag's eyes – said seriously, 'I said I would help in finding the truth. The truth might not be what you want to hear, but that's what I had promised. Not to help you save the culprit.'

Chirag fell silent.

'You do want that, don't you? To find out who did this to your father?'

Chirag replied slowly, 'Yes, of course. I want to find out but –'

'Chirag this is no time to show weakness. If there is something you want to tell me now would be a good time.'

Chirag didn't say anything. That's when Charles decided to leave. He got up and started to walk out of the room. Standing in front of the door he turned around and asked Chirag, 'By the way, did you find your watch?'

'No, I haven't,' Chirag said absentmindedly.

'I see. You don't remember where you could have dropped it?'

'No, I don't, which is odd. I rarely lose things.'

Charles continued to look at Chirag for a few seconds, and then turned around and walked out of the room.

∿

Chitra slumped on her bed when Deepak walked in. He looked at her but didn't say anything. He walked out on to the balcony and stayed there. Chitra waited for a few minutes for him to return, but when he didn't, she went out to talk to him. She had had enough of this; she was not going to take it anymore.

'I want us to leave as soon as this investigation is over,' she declared.

'I don't think that's possible.'

'Why is it not possible?'

'Because I said so – that's why.'

'What is wrong with you?' Chitra shouted, shocked at Deepak's sudden change of attitude.

'Nothing is wrong with me, you have had your way for quite some time. And now it's my turn.'

'I know what this is about. It's that woman isn't it?' She was screaming now.

'Don't bring her into this. She has nothing to do with it,' he shouted back. He turned to walk away when she caught him by the arm and pushed him.

'Oh no, you are not walking away. You want to say something, say it.'

'I don't want to say anything.'

'Why not? She didn't coach you well enough?'

'Stop it Chitra! I'm not going to listen to you badmouthing her. Instead, you should try to learn from her!'

'Learn from her! What? How to destroy other people's marriages?'

'She didn't destroy anyone's marriage.'

Chitra was fuming. At that moment, she felt she could push him off the balcony and not feel bad about it.

Her hands rolled up in a tight fist, she said, 'She is destroying ours.'

'It's all your imagination.'

'Really? Then maybe you can explain as to why you were following her around like a puppy dog.'

Deepak was furious. 'How dare you!'

'Oh, I dare! And it's better for you to beware.'

'Beware of what? What will you do – leave me? Fine, go ahead. I'm not going to stop you.'

Chitra was shocked. 'I can't believe this. She has gotten to you, hasn't she? You are such a fool. Well, I'm not going to give up that easily. She might control your mind, but for how long.'

Deepak didn't want to continue this conversation but he couldn't leave. She was blocking his way. 'Maybe it's best you leave,' he said, but couldn't look into her eyes.

'Are you asking me to leave you?'

'Yes. Isn't it clear?'

'Why?' she blurted out.

'Because, I think it's best.'

'*You* think it's best, or does *she* think it's best.'

'We both feel that it's best.'

'Oh! So it's "we" now…'

'If it makes it easy for you to decide, then yes, we both feel the same. There – I said it.'

'I see, that's why you invited her here. You were planning this all along.'

'No – actually I hadn't. It just happened. And I feel it's for the best.'

'You are blind not to see that she uses you like a toy. She winds you up and there you go gallivanting around like a monkey.'

'That's enough, Chitra. I am not going to be insulted by you anymore.'

'Oh, I don't need to insult you. You've insulted yourself enough – by showing everyone that you have no mind of your own. Her *toy*, that's what you are!'

Deepak pushed her aside so he could leave, but she pushed him back. He lost his balance but supported himself against the railing. She moved closer to him; her face a few inches away from his she looked straight into his eyes and said in a chilly tone, 'If you think you can treat me like dirt then I suggest you wake up because I'm not going to let *anyone* take me for granted. And you tell her for me that this is war and I will not rest till I win.'

She slowly backed away, into the room. Deepak stood dazed for a few seconds in the balcony. Then he slowly walked past her and out of the room. Before leaving he turned around and said, 'It won't be difficult to get you out of here.' He walked out without waiting for a reply.

Chitra's mind was racing with ideas. She was scared, but she was not going to give up without a fight. But she didn't know how, what, she would do.

⌇

Nita stood below Deepak and Chitra's balcony, listening to the fight. She was so engrossed that she didn't notice that Maya had walked into the room behind her.

Maya heard the loud voices as she entered the room. Not wanting Nita to see her she quickly hid behind the heavy silk curtain. After a while the voices stopped abruptly; Nita turned around and slowly walked out of the room.

Maya came out of her hiding place, pleased. Her lips were twisted in a knowing smile, but she quickly composed herself and walked out of the room.

Entering the kitchen she saw constable Rane having a cup of tea and some snacks. Caught by surprise Rane quickly tried to swallow whatever was in his mouth and stood up.

Maya waved her hands and said, 'It's all right, you can finish.'

'No madam, I am okay.'

'I needed a favour from you,' she said, gesturing for him to follow her. Constable Rane quickly walked out of the kitchen behind her. Maya took him to the first floor and whispered some instructions in his ears. He nodded in agreement.

'You understand everything, right?' Maya asked.

'Yes, clearly.'

Maya quietly slipped a five hundred rupee note in his pocket and said, 'There is more where that came from – if you do as I tell you.'

Rane smiled with pleasure. 'You don't worry, I'll take full care,' he said and walked away.

Maya knew this had to end soon or it could turn uglier.

∿

Deepak was agitated. He felt out of control. A part of him was angry that Chitra was right in a way. He had become a toy in the hands of two women. It seemed that his wishes didn't matter much. He didn't even know any longer what he wanted.

Charles caught up with him as he was walking by in a dazed manner.

'Are you all right?' he asked sympathetically. Charles always knew when someone needed a show of sympathy.

'Yes, I'm fine,' Deepak answered.

'You don't look it....'

'Just the pressure of everything.'

'I see. Were you going somewhere?'

'Yes, to the rooftop terrace garden. Just to clear my head.'

'Do you mind if I join you?'

'No, not at all,' Deepak said, without much enthusiasm. He really did want to be alone.

They walked together silently. They reached the garden and Charles said: 'This is really beautiful. I must say, you have a lovely house. And you keep it very well maintained too.'

'Yes, I guess so.... Thanks.'

'You seem a bit distracted. Is everything fine?'

Deepak tried to pull himself together. 'Yes...yes, everything's fine,' he said.

Charles gave Deepak a questioning look. Deepak smiled, 'Well, it seems that you don't believe me.'

'It's hard to, after knowing that you might lie again.'

'Lie again? When did I lie before?'

Charles thought, no wonder he's not successful, he's a bad actor. He looked at Deepak intently, ready to observe his reactions, and said, 'You told us you didn't know Nita was going to be here, but your wife told us it was you who invited her.'

Deepak paled. Trying hard to sound normal, he said, 'I might have, but by accident not intentionally. And I wasn't sure she would actually come. Anyway, she has nothing to do with all this.'

'No, of course not – I didn't say she did. I was wondering why you lied to us. To protect whom or what?'

'I lied to protect Nita. Everyone was already being so cold towards her. If I had told you the truth, you would probably question her and she didn't need that. Now my wife, she couldn't have enjoyed it more – to see Nita troubled. So she did her part.'

'Don't blame her for being a little jealous. I think you should be flattered. A woman like her – so beautiful and honest – actually cares enough to do something. Most would wallow in self-pity.'

'Oh no, she is quite active in such respects,' Deepak said sarcastically.

'You still seem to care for Nita.'

'Well, you cannot just forget someone. They always have a special place – and besides what's so bad in showing a little respect towards others?'

'Oh nothing, as long as respect stays as such, and doesn't turn into something else.'

'What are you trying to say?'

Charles framed each word in his head carefully before he said anything. 'Sometimes old feelings can ruin what you have now, in the present, and by the time you realise it, it's too late to do anything.'

'I see you have been talking to my brother. He's the one filling your head with all this nonsense. He probably told you Nita is the devil. He could never get over the fact that she chose me over him. Always thinking he's the ladies' man. That's why he ran off – couldn't face it – coward. Talking bad about people behind their backs. Trust him to stoop so low....'

'So, your brother is lying?'

'Of course he is!'

'You lie too.'

'To protect –'

'How do you know you are protecting the right person?'

'I just know –'

Charles didn't want to ask anymore questions. He was convinced Deepak was protecting someone – perhaps himself. His explanations had largely been lies – he hadn't told the investigation team one true fact. He would need to prove it or Deepak would get away with it. If only he could see the reason why Deepak was protecting this person.

Charles took his leave and went looking for the inspector.

Chapter 4

Inspector Desai, Charles and Maya were sitting in the library. Inspector Desai was beaming with pride – he had solved the case. He was fairly certain he knew who the culprit was. 'I know who could have done it – at least I have two very strong suspects,' he announced.

Charles and Maya were intrigued. Pleased with their reaction, Desai continued: 'One is Chirag Suri and the other is Sagar Suri. I found out a few more details. It was simple after that. Let me explain it to you – according to your system, the list.'

Charles and Maya both smiled. Each had their own ideas as well.

'Do you have somebody in mind?' Desai asked Charles.

'Yes, I have my doubts about Deepak.'

'And you – who do you think did it?' the inspector turned to Maya.

'My theory is so far-fetched that it's not even worth mentioning at this moment. I have no evidence to back it up.'

Inspector Desai looked at her and said, 'Perhaps your theory is wrong – that's why you have no evidence.'

Maya said with a firm voice, 'No, I'm not wrong. I know I'm right. I just need to prove it.' She said this with so much certainty that for a moment Inspector Desai's confidence staggered.

'You mean to say we are wrong?' he pointed at both himself and Charles.

Maya smiled genially and said, 'No, you are right. Till I prove you wrong.'

Inspector Desai was short of words. He thought, all this time, he had not heard much from her, and now when she speaks, she quietens everyone.

Charles had to jump in. He said, 'Well, inspector – let's discuss the list.'

This brought a smile back on Inspector Desai's face. 'Yes, let's do that. I think we should start with Chirag Suri. I'll go first, tell you all that I found out. Then you can tell me what you have discovered and we can come to a conclusion.'

Charles nodded in agreement.

Inspector Desai began. 'Chirag Suri – the eldest son of Prithvi Suri. Loyal and devoted son, who manages the business single-handedly. Yesterday he finds out that his father intends to give half the business to his youngest brother. All his patience gives out, he loses his balance, goes to his father's room at night, gets into an argument, picks up his walking stick, hits him on the head. Now let's examine the evidence. His alibi is no way near perfect. He had ample opportunity. The prints on the walking stick are not his, but that is child's play these days. His watch was not found on the scene, but like you said, the broken piece of glass did match the watch recovered from Mrs Suri's room. I questioned her again, and she confessed. A motherly instinct – we did know he is his mother's favourite. So we can see Chirag has motive and opportunity, *plus* evidence puts him there.'

'One more thing,' the inspector continued. 'The calls that Mr Suri said he was making from his office – it's a lie. He didn't make any calls. Only one call was made – to us.'

'So it was him who called you?'

'Well, it was his phone that was used to make the call. This implicates him.'

'But why would he call you, if he murdered his father?'

'Yes, but most criminals think they can outsmart the police. They call us, trying to taunt us. But like they say, crime doesn't pay, so sooner or later they get caught. What do you think?' Inspector Desai looked at Maya.

Maya shook her head, 'I think he's too weak to do something like this. But his wife – she could do something like this. She has more audacity.'

'I was going to come to her next. Did you talk to her?' Inspector Desai said.

'Yes, I did,' replied Maya.

'Then perhaps you should summarise what your meeting was like and your impressions of her for us. What do you say Mr Wright?'

Charles nodded in agreement.

'Well, let's see: Aparna Suri, wife of Chirag Suri. Organised, obsessive, judgmental – and completely honest about her opinions about others. She is overly protective of her husband; she comes to his rescue whenever he needs it, perhaps even when he doesn't. She doesn't approve of her father-in-law's choices but doesn't say anything. Only till she finds out that her husband is being victimised and is losing his share. Which I think means more to him than just the finances of it. I think he felt he had lost his father's trust. Anyway, she gets annoyed, goes to talk to her father-in-law at night after her work in the kitchen. He doesn't care much for what she's saying, so she loses her temper – and we know what happened next.'

Maya continued thoughtfully, 'Now the evidence. Her alibi is weak, we know that. She had motive and opportunity. But we don't have anything concrete. So – acquitted on lack of evidence.'

'We can still grill her,' Inspector Desai said. 'She might spill some other details.'

'Oh, yes. Definitely. Actually grill them together – one will surely break.'

The inspector laughed. 'You are ruthless Maya.'

'Only when it's necessary,' she smiled. 'What do you think Charles?'

'It's a good idea.'

'Well then we'll call them together,' the inspector said. 'But for now let's get on with it.' He thought for a few seconds and then said, 'Let's take Deepak next. Would you like to sum him up for us – since you suspect he has a hand in this?'

Charles cleared his throat and said, 'Yes, Deepak Suri, the second oldest brother. Doesn't stay home much. He's a liar – even when he gets exposed he tries to talk his way out of it. Yesterday he found his ex-wife here and is completely enchanted by her. His father has cut off his allowance which gives him motive. Now opportunity: he had plenty, he could easily have come down from the terrace, killed his father and gone back up. Nobody saw him come or go. He said he heard the lamp drop which is another lie – you would not have been able to hear it from that far. That means he was somewhere nearby. Then why did he lie to us? What is he hiding? If he didn't do it, who is he protecting by lying and creating confusion?'

'But we don't have any evidence,' Inspector Desai said.

'Actually we do,' Maya contradicted. 'The Singapore dollar could easily have come from him.'

'You are right!'

'So now we have evidence that puts him on the scene.'

'His whole history with – what's her name, yes, Nita – is also odd. I get all confused,' Inspector Desai said.

'That's because no one tells us anything. They say they don't know. But how can they *not* know. They're hiding something.'

'Maybe it's not very important to us – just some family matter.'

'But that matters. *This* is a family matter. We are the only outsiders apart from the one that ran away. Assuming we are not guilty, that leaves only the family.'

'Yes, you are right. But we cannot probe too much.'

'Why not?'

'Well –'

Maya said, 'Because this is India and we don't like talking about unpleasant family issues here. It's better left unsaid – that's our philosophy.'

'So you'll just brush it aside, never deal with it head on?'

'No, unless circumstances force us to.'

'But isn't that unhealthy?'

'Oh yes. But when generations have been following this system it's not easy to break away. It takes courage to question pre-set norms.'

'The youth of this country doesn't seem so set in convention.'

'Yes, but just changing the way you dress or party is not enough. Has there been a change in the thinking? Now that's a real question that will answer if we have broken out of pre-set conventions or not. I feel there is still a long road ahead.'

Inspector Desai agreed with Maya, 'You are right. There's only been a change from the outside – from the inside we're still the same.'

'I see you're agreeing with me for the first time!'

'Oh no – that's not true,' Desai mumbled.

Maya didn't pursue it and Inspector Desai quickly said, 'Let's move to the next person on the list, Chitra Suri – Deepak Suri's second wife. Married not long ago. They mostly stay away from the house; she didn't want to come back for this function. Doesn't like her husband's ex-wife. Quite natural, I believe.'

'She feels ignored,' added Maya.

'Yes, that's right. She has no motive – unless it's her husband's money being cut off. Opportunity also seems pretty slim. I feel she can be eliminated as a suspect. What do you all think?'

'As a suspect. I think there is no evidence either, but she did give us some vital information.'

'Did you find out anything more?' inquired the inspector.

'Yes I did. Deepak and she were fighting on the balcony of their room and I could overhear them downstairs.'

'What did they say?'

'The gist of it seems to be that he wants to leave her and get back with Nita. But she wouldn't give up easily. She thinks he is being manipulated by Nita. It was a serious fight.'

'Yes, that's serious. So it's gone that far in just a few hours – not even a day yet.' The inspector was surprised at the quick turn of events.

Charles said, 'Then she doesn't have a motive to kill her father-in law, it's more like a motive to kill Nita.'

'Yes, I agree,' replied the inspector.

'So, shall we say she is not a suspect – for now.'

'Yes, I think we can say that.'

'Who's next? Ah, Sagar Suri, youngest son of Prithvi Suri – his favourite. He has an aggressive attitude, carefree – untamed is more like it. His father was partial towards him – so it confuses me why he would do it. Perhaps he needed more money for some new scheme of his, was refused, got angry and lost his cool. When a child who always gets what he or she wants is denied something, it can shock them. His prints were found on the weapon – I just found out. A blood-soaked dinner napkin was found in his room. His visit was unexpected – only his father can confirm if he did in fact write asking him to come home. So all evidence seems to point towards him. And he had the best opportunity. He went to give his father his walking stick; he could have easily killed him and then come back to join you all. It was a good plan but the napkin did him in. He probably didn't think we would look in his room. Lucky for us we found it before he could destroy it.'

The inspector then looked at Maya and Charles and asked, 'Anything you would like to add?'

Maya said, 'I asked him straight if he did it and he said he didn't do it.'

'And you believe him?'

'I don't believe anything unless there's enough proof.'

'Don't you think we have proof enough?'

'Yes, we do – but we still don't have a motive.'

'He'll tell us the motive. I'll make him,' Inspector Desai said.

'But, it would be nice if we knew before.'

'That does help, I won't deny that.'

Charles said, 'Sagar does seem the most obvious person – only his motives are not as obvious.' He looked at Maya and asked, 'You talked to him – what did you find out?'

'Many random things: his fear of turning into his brothers, that's why he keeps running away; his failed relationship with Nita and his dislike for her. He says he would have stopped his brother from marrying her if he had known they were getting married. He thinks his brother doesn't understand him or her.'

'That's true,' Charles said. 'Deepak feels Sagar's jealous of him because Nita chose Deepak instead of him. Feels he was a coward who ran away.'

Maya laughed. 'You see what I meant when I said we don't talk about unpleasant family matters here. If these brothers communicated they would have saved each other so much emotional pain. Misunderstanding, lack of communication, and what do we have – two brothers who don't care much for each other and the women get the advantage.'

Inspector Desai wanted to move on with the investigation so he interrupted before the social debate went further. 'So we can say he is our number one suspect. Until proven otherwise.'

'If you look at the evidence – that's correct.'

'Now the next person in line is Nita Suri –'

'Not a Suri anymore,' corrected Maya and suddenly something clicked in her head. It was all clear to her now. But she needed evidence…where…?

'Yes, you are right,' the inspector continued. 'She is Nita Sharma now – she returned to her maiden name. Married to Deepak for maybe a day or so, vanished, returned after many years causing unpleasantness. But that doesn't mean she would kill. Her alibi is the strongest: Joseph saw her going into her room. Of course she could have left the room and returned without being seen. No evidence, no motive, a strong alibi. She should be excluded from the list of suspects. Her romantic involvements have nothing to do with the murder.'

'I think I'll agree with you,' Charles said. 'Let's move to the next person.'

'Now, this is our last suspect. Sheil Singh – the houseguest. His story was a complete bogus. We found Mr Prithvi Suri's address book, called his friend and found that he has no sons. Only two daughters who are married and living in America. So he lied to the family, moved in here with the intention to rob possibly. He went to Mr Suri's room, found him there, hit him on the head, opened the safe but didn't find anything. So he ran away empty-handed. Nothing else seems to be missing, but the way the papers were lying on the floor it seemed he was looking pretty hard for something. One other thing – the letter we found under the dead body was Sheil's introduction letter. It was a fake of course.'

'He is the only one who was here under false pretences,' Charles said. 'His motive must be something important, otherwise why take such a big risk?'

Maya agreed. 'Yes, I know. Prithvi Suri could have easily called his friend.'

Charles asked the inspector, 'Are we sure nothing valuable is missing?'

'Hundred percent. I even asked the women to check silverware and their personal valuables. Nothing is missing. That does make one wonder. But then a thief acts first then thinks. Perhaps he panicked after killing Prithvi Suri and ran without taking anything.'

'I guess robbery seems the only likely reason. Did you find anything else?'

'Just one other thing, but it's not of much use I think.'

'What is it?'

'Sheil was here in the city for the last one week and was staying at a small hotel before he came here. I've been able to get the hotel guest register here –' the inspector pointed to a register kept on the coffee table. Maya picked it up and started to look through it.

Charles turned to Inspector Desai and said, 'So now if we place our suspects in the order of strongest to weakest, it would be something like this: Sagar Suri, Chirag Suri, Deepak Suri, Sheil Singh, Aparna

Suri, Nita Sharma, Chitra Suri, Asha Suri. Is that right?'

'I would put Sheil before Deepak – that's all,' said the inspector.

'Evidence doesn't put Sheil on the scene – there is evidence that places Deepak on the scene.'

'Yes, true, but Sheil appears more guilty and perhaps has a bigger motive than Deepak.' Just then Inspector Desai's phone rang. 'Yes, yes. Very good work,' he told the person on the other end. 'Yes do that – no delay. Right, fifteen minutes.' He turned to Charles and said, 'Good news at last. We've found Sheil Singh. The idiot bought a ticket at the railway station in that name. We might not be very hi-tech but we do have computers. They've apprehended him and are bringing him here. They should be with us in fifteen minutes.'

'That's very good news. At least some secrets will be revealed.'

Maya looked at inspector and asked, 'Could I take a look at the murder scene – I mean the bedroom? I want to take one last look.'

'Are you looking for something?'

'Well, I don't really know what I'm looking for. But when I find it, I'll call you first.'

'Okay, go ahead,' Inspector Desai said, handing the keys to the room to Maya. As she was leaving the room she picked up the wooden coin that had been found in the bedroom with her.

∿

Maya stood in the middle of Prithvi Suri's enormous room; some people don't even have houses this big, she thought. Her lips curled up in a soft smile. She walked along the passage lined with pillars and noticed all the delicate decorations. She walked over to the French windows; they were all locked. She opened one of them, stepped out and took a quick look.

Then she walked back inside and went over to the desk where Prithvi Suri had been found. Although his body had been taken away soon after he had been found, it felt as if it was still there. Maya walked behind the desk and stood there looking at it directly. Suddenly she turned and her eyes fell on a small table placed against the wall behind the desk. There was an empty space on one corner of the desk where the lamp which Joseph broke had been kept. On the other end was a statue, carved out of wood it was about twelve inches in height – a beautiful piece of art. Maya looked at the statue closely, but she was disappointed. She stood up and surveyed the room again. She moved closer to the desk.

There were many things kept on the desk: personalised stationery, an antique paper weight, a box for cigarettes, a silver tray for letters, and a framed photograph of the whole family. Suddenly something caught Maya's eye. She noticed a small circular indent on top of the cigarette box. She took out the wooden coin and placed it in the indent. It fit perfectly. She applied pressure on it but nothing happened. She stared at the box – she knew she was on the right track. She turned the coin around clockwise. Instantly the coin locked on to some lever and a small drawer slid out of the bottom of the cigarette box.

Maya's heart was racing with the anticipation of what she would find. Gently she took out the little drawer. It was three inches wide, six inches long and nearly an inch deep. Inside was a folded cloth. She opened out the cloth and gazed at the contents. There were nearly fifty or more assorted precious stones – diamonds, sapphires emeralds and rubies.

Maya pulled out the chair and sat down. She picked up the cloth in which the stones were wrapped and looked at it. She smiled with disbelief as she read what was written on the cloth. She placed the stones back in the drawer and shut it, removing the coin from its position. Quickly folding the piece of cloth, she placed it in her pocket, picked up the cigarette box and carried it with her to the library where Charles and Inspector Desai were.

She briskly walked in and placed the wooden cigarette box in the middle of the coffee table. Inspector Desai and Charles both looked at the box and then Maya. 'What is this?' Charles said.

'Our motive.'

'What – how?' the inspector stuttered.

As she picked up the box Maya asked, 'Do you remember this coin that was found in the safe? I kept thinking, why would someone keep a wooden coin in a safe. Obviously, it had to have some importance, otherwise why lock it up. Right?'

Both men nodded in agreement.

Maya picked up the coin and repeated the steps. The drawer opened and she emptied its contents on the table. Both Charles and Inspector Desai were stunned. Inspector Desai took the stones in his palm and inspected them closely, 'Definitely real. Good – no, excellent – quality.'

'Now your robbery idea makes more sense,' Charles said.

'Yes, it does. I knew it.' Inspector Desai felt proud of himself for being the first one who pointed out the robbery angle.

Maya turned to the inspector and said, 'No one mentioned these stones to us. Can you think why?'

The inspector thought for a moment and then shook his head. Charles said, 'There can be only two explanations: they didn't know or they were too scared to tell us.'

'Why? Do you think they have been illegally bought?' asked the inspector.

'Who knows. You'll have to find that out.'

The inspector nodded and returned his gaze to the precious stones.

∿

Sheil – handcuffed – sat in a chair placed in front of Inspector Desai. He was agitated, constantly looking around him in fear.

'Don't look here and there – there is no escape for you.'

'Who wanted to escape?'

'You did. Otherwise why would you run away like this.'

'I didn't run anywhere. I was just leaving the city to travel.'

'Shut up!' Inspector Desai shouted. 'Do you think we are fools? I suggest you start explaining what you were doing here.'

'I was visiting my father's friends. They asked me to stay for the festival and I accepted –'

'The truth! We've spoken to your supposed father Kamal Singh.'

Sheil knew he was trapped.

'I want the truth,' Inspector Desai continued. 'Otherwise we do have other ways of getting you to talk….' Inspector Desai gave Sheil a threatening stare. Inspector Desai's threat worked. Sheil started to speak in a single breath.

'I am not Kamal Singh's son. But I knew him well at one time – used to work for him. Now try to and put yourself in my place. I had worked and saved for a few years intending to travel to Bali with my earnings. When I reached there everything was beautiful and warm. Then one day, while I was on this group tour, I saw this woman – Nita. She was so lovely, gentle and delicate: I fell for her immediately. I talked to her and we became friendly. As she was leaving, I decided not to let go of her so easily. I was on a vacation and following her would be an adventure, I thought. I followed her to Singapore and then here. I'd heard of Mr Prithvi Suri, I knew all about him. Mr Singh often talked about him and said what a character he was. Well, the idea came to me suddenly. I would pretend to be Mr Singh's son. I knew they had lost touch some time ago and I figured Mr Suri wouldn't call to verify what I was saying. Anyway, I felt it was worth a try. The old man greeted me in the friendliest manner and at once asked me to come and stay here for a few days. I accepted.'

When Sheil paused, the inspector abruptly said, 'Go on. That's not all, is it?'

'No, it isn't. You see inspector, I had come here following the woman of my dreams. But when she saw me, she pretended not to know me at all. This really broke my heart. All this trouble and risk that

I had taken was of no use in the end. She didn't feel the same way towards me as I felt towards her.

'She ignored me and avoided me the whole day. Then, when we went into the living room after dinner, I overheard Deepak Suri telling her to meet him on the terrace. This really infuriated me. That very second I decided it was best that I leave immediately. I do have some self-respect. But I didn't want to leave so abruptly either. I went to my room and thought I would wait for everyone to go to bed and then leave quietly.'

'Did you follow her to the terrace?'

'Yes, I did. I had to hear what they said with my own ears.'

'What did you hear?'

'He told her how much he still loved her and that he would leave his wife in a second if she would just come back to him.'

'And what did she say.'

Sheil was uncomfortable. He didn't want to repeat this part of the conversation. It was painful.

'Yes?'

'She said she had been a fool before. She was immature, a child. She had realised over time that she loves him, but she would never break his marriage. That's all I heard. After this I just walked back to my room and stayed there till midnight. Then I left quietly.'

'So you didn't go into Mr Prithvi Suri's room?'

'Actually I did. I went to get my letter. I didn't want anyone to find it. I could really get into trouble with that. When I went in... what I found was too terrible. I couldn't think straight. I ran out of there and went straight to the train station. My fake identity would have made me a suspect right away. Anyway I didn't really do it, so it didn't matter if I was here or not. You can find out about me from my employers in Canada. They will vouch for my character – I'm no thief or convict.'

'That can be easily verified. Until then, I suggest you go back to your room and stay there till I call you.'

Inspector Desai asked the constable to take Sheil's handcuffs off and escort him to his room. He then turned to Charles and said, 'I guess you were right. It doesn't seem like he did this.'

'May I suggest something?' Maya said.

'Sure, please go ahead,' Inspector Desai said. He had newfound respect for her. She was a silent worker and showed results – he admired that.

'I suggest we gather everyone in this room and tackle each one individually. The truth will definitely come out.'

'You are sure?'

'Yes, I know who did it.'

Inspector Desai exclaimed, 'What? Who?'

'Oh no, not now. I want to confirm something first. Though I do want you to do something.' Maya shared her idea with the men and left the room. To get confirmation, she said.

Chapter 5

Inspector Desai looked around at the circle of faces. Mrs Asha Suri looked pale and worn out. Chirag and Aparna both looked strangely docile, Chitra was sitting up stiffly; Deepak was slumped next to her. Nita was there, sitting in a chair set slightly apart from the rest of the family. And Sagar looked defiant.

Inspector Desai thought, what am I supposed to do now? One should be careful in doing favours! He said, 'To begin with, I must tell you all that we know who the killer is but we won't tell you yet. You see there are certain facts that need clarification first. Only then will we be able to tell you everything more precisely. Instead of calling you'll one by one, we decided to do this together. Saves us all time and then we can all get on with our day. Now let's start.

'There is a case against every person here. We will, Mr Chirag Suri, begin with the case against you. You had no love for your father! You respected him, feared him, but did not love him. You were obedient and dutiful for the sake of this empire your father had created, which you thought you would inherit one day. On the day of his death he had cut your share in half and given it to your brother. You knew that on his death you would probably inherit a substantial share. You must have known this because your mother knew – and you are her favourite. There is the motive. After dinner you say you went to phone your friends and associates. You did call, but not your friends – you called the police. You didn't make any other calls. Before making a call to us you could have easily gone to your father's room and killed him. In this scuffle your wristwatch fell on the floor by the desk and the glass broke. We found the fragments on the scene. You probably panicked and didn't realise. But your mother saw it. She pretended to faint and carried the watch out of the room with her. This is why you kept insisting that the murder was done by someone on the outside.

You wanted us to look elsewhere. You would have gotten away with it had it not been for the watch fragment.'

Chirag started to say something, but Desai held up his hand, cutting him short. He turned to Aparna. 'Madam, you too had a motive. You are intensely protective of your husband and unhappy with the fact that his life was completely governed by his father's wishes. On the day of his death, your father-in-law had done something that made an impact on your husband. You became furious and decided to talk to your father-in-law about it. After the dinner you went into the kitchen – part of your daily routine – and then left. You lied to us about the amount of time you were there. We know you only spent fifteen minutes there, and the rest of the time before you returned to the living room hasn't been explained. You could have easily gone to your father-in-law's room. Both of you got into an argument; you lost control and attacked him, killing him. After this you went back to the kitchen. You needed a drink of water. After which you could have used your husband's office phone to call us. Then you went to the living room and joined the others. There is also one other possibility: you and your husband were in this together. He does the deed while you help him take care of all the details. But madam – you forgot the watch.'

'None of this is true,' Aparna said quietly.

'Well then you did it alone – to protect your husband from being hurt again by his father. You are thoroughly capable.'

'I didn't kill him.'

'As the inspector said,' Charles intervened, 'there is a case against everyone except Ms Nita, Mrs Chitra Suri and Mrs Asha Suri. The rest had motive and opportunity.'

Inspector Desai continued, 'Then there is Mr Deepak Suri. You were always a problem child, always needing your father's help. On the day of his death your father had cut off your allowance – or was it more like shopping money? Even you knew that on his death you would probably inherit a suitable amount to do what you pleased. There is the motive. After dinner you spent a little time in the living room and went straight to the rooftop terrace. You could have easily left the terrace, gone down to your father's room and killed him. You left the room – but in your panic you dropped a Singapore dollar coin. You did not go back to the terrace, because you see, you couldn't have heard the lamp break or Joseph's cry from there. We checked. You were waiting for the right time to come out and you came in last. You had motive and ample opportunity. You would have got away with it had it not been for the Singapore dollar that you dropped.'

Deepak too was in a shock. This was not what he had expected.

'I was on the terrace – that's the truth.'

'Can you prove it? Was there someone there with you?'

Deepak didn't say anything. Inspector Desai was enjoying this now – it was true that they broke under this kind of pressure.

'If you won't tell us, I'll have to –' the inspector paused. Seeing that Deepak was not going to say anything, he turned to Nita and said, 'All right then. Ms Nita, would *you* mind telling us?'

Nita was pale and silent.

'No? Okay then. I'll do the telling. Mr Deepak Suri asked Ms Nita here to meet on the terrace. That's why you were there, right? And please don't lie this time. I have a witness.'

Deepak quietly bowed his head and said, 'Yes, we met for a few minutes.'

'Good, that wasn't too difficult, was it? This does give you an alibi but not for a long time. You still had time to go and do the crime. You are still not off the hook.'

'I didn't kill my father,' Deepak said.

Chirag finally found his voice. 'How can you say things like this. How dare you suggest that we killed our own father?'

Sagar interrupted his brother. In an amused tone he said, 'Let him go on, I am next. We are being tested, soon we'll see who turns out to be positive.'

Chirag looked at his brother distastefully. 'Can you ever be serious? Is this a joke to you?'

'Oh god! Do you always have to be so uptight?'

Chirag murmured softly, 'We'll see if you find it funny when they catch you.'

Inspector Desai smiled at them. 'Now all this could be an act too. You and your brother are not on good terms – everyone knows that. But suppose you both – tired of being at the mercy of your father – decided to get rid of him? Sagar, you come home after a long period of time. Chirag resents your presence. He shows contempt and anger towards you. You on the other hand degrade him; make fun of his docile behaviour. Then comes the night of the murder. One of you goes and does the crime, the other goes after some time and leaves evidence just to confuse us. Now perhaps all three are involved – a coin dropped to confuse us even more.'

Chirag sprang up, 'What the hell are you talking about?'

'Please Mr Suri, calm down. I'm only stating the possibilities! Which is true we'll know soon. Now let's deal with you Mr Sagar Suri. There is a very strong case against you. To begin with, you were your father's favourite. Whatever you asked for, whenever you asked, from wherever you asked – you got it. He never said no to you. On the day of his death you arrived unexpectedly and on the same day your father gave you half your brother's share. Now we assumed that you were happy with this, but what if you weren't? Maybe your father gave you a choice – either this or nothing. You probably knew that on his death you would inherit a considerable share which could be more suitable to you. After dinner you took Maya for a guided tour and when you came back you went to give your father his walking stick. Instead of giving it to him, you used it to kill him. Then you quickly wiped the blood from your hands in a dinner napkin, threw it in the dustbin in your room – which we found by the way – and went back to the living room. Your prints have been found all over the murder weapon. Do you have anything to say?'

'Only one thing. Why would I kill my father if he was giving me a share of his money?'

'You can tell us better, since you're the one who did it.'

'I didn't do it. You are wrong, very wrong.'

'I'm sorry Mr Suri but the evidence speaks for itself.'

'What about that guest Sheil? You haven't even bothered to look for him. It could have been him.'

'He is innocent. We found him and know why he came here. He's not the son of your father's friend. He lied just to get into this house because of Ms Nita for whom he has strong feelings. But when he realised she didn't care for him, he packed his bags and left.'

'That doesn't mean he didn't kill our father.'

'He is not a thief or a convict, he is respectable citizen who let his emotions carry him away. Besides there is no evidence that puts him on the crime scene. He didn't steal anything either – so that wasn't his motive. So he is not a suspect anymore.'

There was deathly silence. All the commotion and protests had died down. They watched the inspector as he slowly began to speak again. 'It is all here you see. No one can deny the facts and if there is anything that is not clear, you will do that for me.'

No one said anything. Everyone in the room was terrified of the consequences the inspector was predicting.

When nothing was said, Inspector Desai got up and signalled to his men standing at the door. They went straight to Sagar Suri and asked him to come with them. Sagar looked at the inspector and then at his brothers. Suddenly his fear was clearly visible in his eyes.

Chirag Suri got up and said, 'Inspector, you are making a mistake. My brother might be everything but he is not a criminal.'

'There is nothing, I can do. It would be best for him to confess.' He signalled to his men with a nod to take Sagar away.

Just as they were about to walk out, Maya walked in. She walked up to the circle of people sitting in silence and said, 'Oh, it seems I missed everything.'

Inspector Desai looked at her, waiting for her to continue. It had all been planned before. Maya turned to Sagar and said, 'I told you – they'll get you.'

Sagar's mouth was set in a grim line. Maya asked the inspector, 'If you don't mind I would like to present a theory of mine to everyone –'

'Of course, please go ahead. I think we could all hear something new.'

Maya said to Sagar, 'Why don't you listen too?' She waved him back to his chair.

'Now, let's see.' She looked around at everyone and began, 'It is all here. Usually in a crime there is a victim, a perpetrator and one most important fact that links them – the motive. Now let's start with the victim – Prithvi Suri, the head of the family. What kind of man was Prithvi Suri – strong-willed, intelligent, always in control. He always did what he wanted: but even though he was a control freak he was not a mean person. He helped his children, took care of all their needs and so on. So how is it that he was caught unaware like this. Who would want to harm him and why?

'Prithvi Suri was not only in control always, he was also thorough. We can see that by the fact that he had already decided which of his sons would get what, even though he kept threatening to do otherwise. He was a good judge of character: I don't know, if any of you have read his will. I have – I'll tell you about it a little later.

'Now we come to the murderer – the person who committed this crime. It was evidently not an accident. The victim was beaten repeatedly. That meant whoever did this did not want to take any chances. This then rules out robbery and death by accident. So I had to ask myself – who would want him dead, for whom is this beneficial. Nearly all of you benefit from his death. It's most beneficial to you Chirag. But before making any assumptions, I wanted to look at this from another angle. Usually in a crime within a family the family member's psychology comes into play. Their inner politics – everything becomes important. Keeping all this in mind, I was convinced that the murder was committed by a person closely connected with the deceased.

'In my judgment, only two people fit this description: Aparna Suri and Deepak Suri. Chirag I rejected because he is a person who would not be able to take the pressure of killing someone. He would be a wreck. But you did go to your father's room, didn't you?

'Chitra I rejected because of two reasons: the first was common sense. She could never have made it up the stairs, kill Prithvi Suri and walk back down quickly without tripping at least once or twice. It was the dress you wore – you complained yourself while going up the stairs the first time we went. It was difficult for you to walk, your shoes kept getting caught in your dress. So for you it could not have been physically possible. Another reason why you can't be the killer is because it's not in your nature to attack from behind. You are a straightforward person. You face all your battles head on. And to sneak up from behind and attack someone would just not suit you. If you ever had to kill someone you would probably shoot them straight in the heart. Am I right?'

Chitra started to laugh, 'Yes, that's true. That's exactly how I would do it.'

Maya said, 'You see, a person's nature has a lot to do with their behaviour. And now Sagar. He was a difficult case with all the evidence pointing directly at him. Even with his arrogant and careless attitude, I was sure he was not a confident person. He shies away from responsibility not because he can't commit but because he lacks confidence in himself. He can live in any condition but not with broken pride. He won't risk being caught – that's why he wouldn't do it. Also, having his father alive and well would be more worthwhile for Sagar than having his father dead. Killing him would bring him no gain.

'This leaves me with two members of the family. Aparna Suri and Deepak Suri. Let's talk about you Deepak. First, you are a person who I've noticed doesn't have much say in anything. In a way, your situation is worse than Chirag. For years you have been the neglected one. The eldest was your mother's favourite, the youngest, your father's. That leaves you with no attention. All your wants and needs were taken care of but you lacked attention. You had learned to accept your fate, but perhaps after years and years of festering discontent, you snapped. Moreover it is possible you had a secret grudge against your brother – which might have led you to plant evidence that incriminates him. It is simple, if you think about it. You had plenty of time to go and kill your father, and you have been lying to us from the beginning. At first I thought you were protecting someone, but it was not someone, it was yourself who you were trying to protect. Sometimes it is the quiet ones that are often prone to sudden and unexpected anger. You fit the profile well.

'The other person that I considered was Aparna Suri – she is capable of taking the law into her own hands if she feels it is the right thing to do. She is the type who would judge and execute without any hesitation. Mind you she doesn't do this for selfish reasons. It's for someone else or for the common good. She's organised, methodical, hence she could have planned this in advance. And she found a good scapegoat when Sagar showed up unexpectedly. And the fact that his presence meant more harm to her husband only strengthened her ideas.

'And now, having come so far, I examined the circumstances of the crime itself. Now take yourselves back to the scene of the crime. The first thing that struck me was the mess around the safe. Prithvi

Suri's body lay on the desk but nothing had been touched there. Only the items in the safe had been scattered around. Perhaps someone had killed him for the sake of robbery – or to try and indicate that the motive was robbery. But a thief never touches only a safe. When nothing was found in the safe, he or she should have checked other drawers, other places in the room where valuables could be stored. Another point, if it was an outsider, how did he know where to find Prithvi Suri's locker combination. That means someone in-house was responsible. So if it was not robbery, then why were the items of the safe scattered everywhere. It could only mean one thing – someone was looking for something. Now what could that something be? According to you all there was nothing stolen from the safe. This troubled me. Either you all know what was in that safe or were hiding the truth. In either case there is something that might be missing from the safe.

'But this idea was just an empty idea without concrete evidence. The second extraordinary point was the way Prithvi Suri was murdered – he was hit repeatedly. Which goes to show that it's not someone with too much strength.

'It would not have made any impression on me if Joseph hadn't mentioned something again. Even he saw what most of us failed to see — it was intentional.

'Now let's examine the evidence one by one. The walking stick has Sagar's prints and the victim's blood; fragments of Chirag's watch have been found along with a Singapore coin which belongs to Deepak and a letter of introduction that Sheil brought with him. Now this evidence implicates all the male members of the family. The blame will definitely fall on at least one of you; which one will depend on fate, while the murderer goes free. These issues just didn't make sense, yet they were all there. This crime was becoming more and more incomprehensible. It didn't have any order — the pieces of the puzzle were not fitting.

'And then it suddenly dawned on me — we are looking at this from a point of view that the murderer wanted Prithvi Suri dead. What if this were not so? What if Prithvi's murder had to take place to necessitate something else? You could say there is nothing in this theory, but yet it is not so. He had to be a liability for someone and it was time for him to go. And I get this feeling that there is nothing about this crime that is absurd. On the contrary, it is a well-planned and admirably carried out crime. Therefore everything that has happened here up till now was meant to happen...

'I decided to go over it once again right from the beginning – and I saw my first glimmer of light. I finally came to two valuable clues in this case – both are connected and when we find that connection we'll have our killer.

'Now the first is that evidence points to everyone and everyone has a weak alibi. And the second clue is the robbery that did or did not take place. Since we didn't find anything missing we assumed nothing was stolen. But something was – what and by whom?

'Since there is evidence to prove all of you were there at one point or another – except Chitra and Nita – who wants to tell me what they took? If you won't, I'll have to.'

No one spoke up. Maya shook her head and continued. 'Well let me tell you what I thought. I figured that perhaps Sheil Singh took something. After all he's the one who ran away, right?'

Everyone nodded in agreement. Maya signalled to the constable by the door and he opened the door. Sheil walked in. Chirag shouted at him, 'You liar! Get out of this house!'

Maya quietly interrupted him, 'Don't you want to know the truth?'

Chirag sat down grumbling. Sheil moved quietly to one side and sat down as far away as possible from Chirag. Maya stood right in front of Sheil and studied his face. Then she asked him, 'Tell me Sheil – who are you? And don't tell me you are not Kamal Singh's son. We know that. I want to know whose son you are. Because Prithvi Suri would not have let a stranger stay in his house if he didn't have an idea. He could have easily found out about you – like we did. By the way, we do have tests now that can prove it....'

Sheil's face had lost all its colour. He got to his feet. Maya continued. 'That was the real reason why you came here, wasn't it? Not that pretty romantic story that you told us. You had decided to come here before you met her. Coming to see what kind of a man your father was....'

Sheil slumped in his chair. His voice broken and heavy, he said, 'Yes, it's true. I've always wondered....

Mother spoke about him sometimes. They knew each other in college, that's how I knew about Kamal Singh. I grew up with an obsession to see my father, what he was like. I made a bit of money and decided to come here. I wasn't going to let him know who I was. I didn't want anything from him. I only wanted to see the man who was my father....'

Inspector Desai said in almost a whisper, 'God, I've been so blind.... I can see it now, same height, physique – the uncanny likeness to the rest of the family.'

Sheil continued as if the inspector had not said anything, 'But the rest is the truth. I was leaving that night and went to take my letter. That's when I saw him – it terrified me. If you found out I was his son I would definitely be blamed for the murder.'

'So you ran. If you didn't take anything and I know why the rest of these people were in that room, then who did? This only leaves two people. One is Chitra and the other Nita. As I said, I don't think Chitra would have been able to make it up the stairs so it leaves you, Nita. You stole something from that safe didn't you?'

Up till now Nita had felt secure. The sudden accusation made her feel like a deer stunned by the headlights of a car. 'No.... I didn't take anything,' she stammered.

'Yes, you did and you killed Prithvi Suri for it!' Maya shouted at her.

'No, no – I didn't find –'

Maya looked at her and smiled. Everyone was listening intently – in awe.

'Of course you didn't find it. It wasn't there.'

Maya slowly pulled out a long white envelope, took out a set of documents and showed it to her. 'Is this what you were looking for?'

Nita got up to grab the papers. 'Give me – give me that,' she said. Before she could get to the papers, however, Constable Rane had already moved quietly behind her and caught hold of her. She shouted and struggled with the constable to let her loose.

'You cannot prove I did it.'

Maya handed the papers to Inspector Desai who quietly began reading them.

'Actually I can,' Maya said to Nita.

Nita stared at her, her eyes burning with hate and anger. Now – at this moment – her true self was visible. Her façade had disappeared and her true nature revealed.

Maya went to the door, opened it and picked up something from the floor. She walked back to a table kept in the middle of the room and from a brown bag took out a rock slightly rectangular in shape. She said, 'This is the murder weapon.' She turned it slightly to one side and showed the bloodstains on it. 'I'm sure you'll find her prints on it.'

Nita was quickly taken away by the police.

Everyone in the room was too bewildered to show any reaction. After a while someone spoke, 'How did you know she did it?'

'Yes, please explain. How?'

∿

A sense of relief had descended on the room by now. Maya had asked that tea be served first before she explained how she had discovered that Nita was the murderer. Everyone had settled down now, a cup of tea in their hands.

'Go on, tell us from the beginning,' Inspector Desai said. He was baffled. He had only seen this done in the movies.

178

Maya was more than pleased to explain. 'Let's see – where to begin... Yes, let's start with the sequence of events. Prithvi Suri was attacked, then killed. Then the murderer went over to the safe, opened it, looked for something and then left. Now you'll have to tell me the truth. Let's begin with you Chirag. You were one of the first few suspects. There was evidence to show that you were in the room. Were you not there at some point?'

Chirag replied slowly. 'Yes. I went up to see my father. And to talk to him in private about his decision about the business. I found him like that – dead. It was a shock. I stepped back in such a way that my ankle twisted and I fell. That's when I think my watch fell out. I didn't realise it though. I walked out of the room and went straight to my office.'

Maya looked at Aparna and said, 'You saw him go into his study and followed him, didn't you?'

Aparna said, 'Yes, it's so stupid not to have told you. I didn't do it, but I was scared.'

'I know, that's why you tried to throw suspicion on as many people as you could, but in that you did give me much information. One detail you said made me really think. You said Deepak followed Nita like a puppy dog. And I thought what if he was not following her but watching her instead. Then there are other things you said which made me wonder a bit more: "she brings bad news" for instance. It only meant your subconscious was sensing something negative about her. So do you want to tell us your side of the story?'

'Yes. I saw Chirag come down the stairs. He looked ... nervous –'

'Agitated is the word you're looking for.'

'Yes, that's it. It looked as if he had done something that had upset him. I quickly assumed he must have gone to his father to talk and that it probably didn't go well. It maddened me so I decided, enough is enough. I walked upstairs to give my father-in-law a piece of my mind. When I reached his room, I saw him there – dead. I didn't know what to do, or think. I quickly walked out and went to the kitchen for a drink. I was so afraid to tell anyone, in case Chirag had done it. I decided it best to keep out of it and let someone else discover it. I didn't know what else to do.'

'You feared it was Chirag who killed his father. That's why you kept protecting him by confusing us, making us think it was you. As long as we stayed confused, the fewer the chances of us ever solving the crime. You had us going for a while. On the whole you pointed me to Nita. Sagar did try to tell us too, but we thought his judgment could be emotionally motivated, so I didn't take it seriously. But before we get to him, let's talk about Deepak. Now this was most interesting. Your history with Nita fascinated me and what seemed odd to me was that no one knew anything about anything. Now that was not normal; there is always a reason – it could be a humiliating reason but there is still always a reason. At first I thought you were lying but then later another idea struck me: what if you really didn't know – she didn't give you a reason. Only that made sense. But why, why won't she tell you? In the end I realised that to figure this crime out I need to first figure out this woman. Deepak, I think, was the only one who suspected she was involved, but he was not sure, right?'

'Yes, I had my doubts. We had met on the terrace for only a few minutes – perhaps five or ten – and she had left me there. She could have easily done this. But I couldn't be sure why.'

'I'll tell you why – but first I'll have to explain the history. This is just what I think and you are more than welcome to correct me if I'm wrong. Nita was involved with Sagar first, then one day their courtship ended. We are led to believe she is the one who left Sagar to be with Deepak. But all of it is not true. Sagar left her and she then got involved with Deepak. Deepak having been the docile one found himself flattered at the idea that his brother's woman was interested in him. She knew how to play him – you fell for her and they decided to marry. And I'm sure she's the one who made the suggestion indirectly. The cruel truth is that she never cared for you much – your wife was right, she was using you because she was still in love with Sagar and all this was done just to get some reaction out of him. She probably thought he would stop her and so on and so forth. But that didn't happen. Sagar couldn't have cared less. He didn't even know about the wedding. Her plans failed – that's why she ran away, vanished. Except she didn't vanish – the French police found her after a few months and your father was contacted. They have it on record which is how I found out. He even went to see her. He was an experienced man and knew why she had done what she did so he offered her a way out — divorce and a financial settlement. She signed the papers, and has waited all these years to execute her revenge. And after so many years she got her opportunity.'

'You mean to say she hated our father so much that she did this?'

'Oh no! She didn't hate your father. He was not the real victim. The victim was your brother — Sagar!'

Sagar was stunned. 'What! Me? Why?'

'Why! Do you really have to ask? The most common crime is the crime of passion — not for money. A rejected woman, a dejected woman can become a very dangerous woman. She hated you with the same passion that she loved you. She would have gotten away with her plan too, had it not been for Deepak's sudden rekindling of old feelings. It was better than she had hoped — she could get Deepak and at the same time get rid of the person who could spoil her chances. Now the only problem was the divorce papers that she had signed — she needed them destroyed. On her way back from the terrace she killed your father and searched his safe for the papers. Lucky for us she didn't find them there.'

'Where were they?' Deepak asked.

'Your father had given it to your mother saying that it was a copy of his will. She never checked — but I checked today and found the divorce papers instead of the will. It was as clear as daylight.'

'I had a hunch,' Deepak said quietly.

'Yes, I know. That's the reason why you kept close to her and this was a good pretext. After the murder your suspicions were aroused and you pretended to want to leave your wife — a fine performance by the way — your wife believed you.'

'Yes, I was scared. I thought if she had done it, Chitra could be the next victim. To keep her safe I had to tell her to leave. But she wouldn't listen.'

'Yes, I overheard you both from downstairs. Nita was there, and so was I, hiding behind the curtains.'

Sheil, who had been silent for a while now, spoke gently: 'How did you find out about me?'

'It was just a wild guess. You had an uncanny resemblance to Sagar — which I had noted at the dinner table. I decided to bluff. If it was true, great, if not, even then I would have created a doubt in everyone's minds. I needed the effect that this statement would have. I needed Nita to be rattled a bit. She ignored you when you got here, so when she found out you are also their brother, she would regret what she had done, and I could surprise her. And it worked.'

Sagar shivered and said: 'If she had gotten away with it.... I don't even want to imagine what could have happened!'

'Oh it would have been disastrous. Once a person kills, it's not difficult to do again and again. They lose respect for life itself.'

'What made you think she did it?'

'Oh, that credit goes to Joseph. He wanted to know how Mr Suri was killed. When I told him he was appalled by how someone could hit him again and again on his head like that. He acted it out and that made me think of the word hammered and that reminded me of a conversation I'd had. When all the women were told by the inspector to go down and wait in the living room, Nita had said "Poor old man, hammered to death". How did she know he was beaten several times? Unless she's the one who did it. She had hit him with a stone, dabbed same blood on the walking stick to make it look like the murder weapon because it had Sagar's prints all over it. She left the room with the rock, dropped the napkin in Sagar's room and kept the rock in the garden, among one of the piles that are randomly placed all over. It doesn't take too long and the random placement of rocks only helps. I have to give credit to Sagar for my finding the rock. When I saw you looking around the garden and bushes around the rocks, I thought to look up on the terrace.'

'Very good! I must say Maya, that was brilliant. I could never have thought out things in so much detail!' Inspector Desai applauded her, truly impressed by her detailed characterisation and analysis.

'Thank you,' Maya smiled.

'I think we should be getting along now,' the inspector said, and then recalled the gems they had found. Turning towards Chirag, he said, 'Oh yes! Mr Suri, we found this in your father's cigarette box. You can keep them for now and do as you please. When I need them to make my report I'll ask you.' The inspector handed him the stones, said his goodbyes and walked out.

⌣

Charles and Maya were having breakfast before planning their next move. Charles said, 'Inspector

Desai seemed smart – at least he was smart enough to know whom to take help from. He will be successful in his career!'

Maya laughed, 'No, he won't.'

'Why?'

'Because he is not your conventional policeman. He's the type who is open to adopting new ideas, techniques – and that is unfortunately not acceptable. Don't look so shocked,' she said, noticing Charles' expression. 'It is like this everywhere. A person who goes against convention experiences much resistance.'

'Anyway, you let him take all the credit!'

Maya placed her elbows on the table, moved a little forward and said softly, 'If we have to set up a base here, it would be nice to have friends in the right places.'

'Well that is what we went for – didn't work out as planned!'

'Who says?'

Charles raised his eyebrow.

Maya had finished eating. She removed her plate and cleared the area in front of her. Then she took out the folded piece of cloth and opened it up gently.

Charles came forward and looked at it.

'It looks like some ancient text. We'll have to get it deciphered.'

'It looks like a mixture of different languages.'

'Where did you find this?'

'The precious stones in the box were wrapped in it.'

Charles was glad Maya was on his team. 'It has been four years now since we started the Black Spiders, and we still have a long way to go. The annual meeting will be in a few months and we must be fully operational by then.'

'We will be,' she replied with full confidence. She recalled the Black Spiders manifesto:

BLACK SPIDERS
Project 192/192

Base in all the countries of the world. No matter how dangerous or how unbearable the conditions, they would be there. The vision that motivates the Spiders is their common passion for preserving life on this planet. They will go to any extent to do this. The only act they never do is to take life for their cause. They knew the minute they disrespect their cause by doing just the opposite of what they believe in they will lose, and they cannot afford to lose. Their presence is the only element that can bring a little hope. Their purpose is too great to be cut short in the middle by guns.

∿

'When are you leaving to deposit this?' Charles asked.

'Tonight, I've already booked a charter plane. I'll be back by tomorrow.'

'We'll have the translation by then too.'

'Oh yes. Guaranteed.'

'How long do you think it will take to set up base here?'

'Six months, max.'

'Hmmm... then we have no choice but to stay here for six months.'

'Well for me it's great – it's home. For you it'll be an experience.'

'You know I don't mind new experiences.'

'When I come back we'll find you a much homelier place to stay. The hotel will be too boring.'

∿

Chirag and Aparna Suri were taking a walk in the garden. All the funeral formalities were over and the guests had left.

Chirag was saying, 'You really thought I did it?'

Aparna was a little embarrassed for being so wrong. 'Yes, I did. You would have thought the same if you had seen me like that.'

Chirag said thoughtfully, 'Perhaps you're right. You were sweet − trying to protect me.'

'You know I always protect you. But sometimes one has to protect oneself.'

'Who needs to when I have you?' Chirag threw his head back and laughed.

∫

Sagar walked towards them, saying, 'Well, goodbye.' He stood beside Aparna with one arm around her. She stiffened a little but quickly relaxed. Sagar laughed and said, 'You still don't like me?'

'No that's not true. I was wrong − I should be trying harder.'

'I was just pulling your leg. I have a rotten sense of humour obviously! Anyway, I'm leaving now − all the formalities are over and I am off to Hawaii with

Sheil. He's a nice boy, and it will give us a chance to bond. After all he is a part of our family. I've always wanted to live in Hawaii for some time, if I had a bit of money.'

'I hope you enjoy yourself,' Chirag said.

'Sorry if I made life a little difficult for you,' Sagar said rather awkwardly.

'I should be more patient with you. It's not all your fault,' Chirag said.

'Maybe you two should come and visit me. A vacation that you can plan. Freedom to choose – right? Well, bye then.'

∫

'You were ready to throw me out, just to protect me,' Chitra said.

'Yes, I would have. Even if I had to drag you out of here myself. I didn't trust her.'

'And I was so angry with you – harbouring all sorts of horrible notions about you. I am so sorry.'

'Don't be, how could you have known.'

She said after some thought, 'Maybe we should stay here and spend some time at home.'

'I was thinking the same. If you want we can get our own place. It won't be as big as this, but it will be ours.'

Chitra was excited, this would be a new beginning for them....